TANGI'S TEARDROPS

TANGI'S TEARDROPS

By Liz Grace Davis

TANGI'S TEARDROPS

Liz Grace Davis
(Elizabeth Grace T. Adewole)
Copyright © 2012
All Rights Reserved.

AUTHOR'S NOTE

This book is a work of fiction. Names, characters, places and incidents are products of the author's imagination or are used fictitiously. Any resemblance to actual events or locales or persons, living or dead, is entirely coincidental.

The scanning, uploading and distribution of this book via the internet or any other means without the permission of the publisher is illegal and punishable by law. Please purchase only authorized electronic editions, and do not participate in or encourage electronic piracy of copyrighted materials. Your support of the author's rights is appreciated.

Contact **Liz Grace Davis** via email at
Liz_Davis1@yahoo.com

Cover art by **Tamra Westberry**

Layout provided by **Everything Indie**
http://www.everything-indie.com

This novel is dedicated to my mother, Laimi:
"Otji, you'll always be my pleasure at home."
I love you so much.

Acknowledgements

Thanks to my husband, Toye, for believing in me every step of the way. I couldn't have done this without your love and support. You're my rock and I love you more than you can imagine. I always will.

I want to thank all my family and friends. I'm blessed to have you all in my life.

Thanks to my writing friends for traveling this journey with me. Larissa Hinton, for holding my hand and for pushing me sometimes when I wanted to give up. Tammy Barley, for teaching me a lot of what I know about writing. Monterey and Misty, for believing in this book from the first page to the last. You all helped make this book a reality.

Chapter One
Final Goodbye

A crisp chill from the rain-washed air streamed in through the village church's door. It penetrated Tangi's thin, black cotton dress and cooled her back as she limped behind her family down the aisle toward the front pews.

It had all happened too fast. One minute she could hear her Papa's deep throated laughter, his soothing voice telling her goodnight as he tugged her threadbare blanket up to her chin.

Two Sundays ago they had been here at the church. All of them; one of the few Sundays Papa didn't have to work and could accompany Tangi and her two older stepsisters, Nona and Maria. None of them had known it would be the last time he would enter alive.

Two days after that, he had caught cerebral malaria—and five days later, he was gone. And Tangi had become an orphan.

Her mother had died shortly after she was born. For twelve years Papa had not only been both father and mother to her, but also her best friend. One of the few people who looked at her and didn't just see her disability.

The insides of Tangi's stomach twisted into a tight knot as she gazed at the plain wooden coffin in front of the church. She wished she could flap it open and beg Papa to wake up. But she was back in the small church to say goodbye to him for the last time.

The church was not the same anymore. The cross-shaped wooden clock ticked from the wall at the far end of the altar, as if nothing significant had happened. To her, every minute that passed was another minute further away Papa was gone.

Every Sunday, Pastor Markus lit two beeswax altar candles and placed them on both sides of a bouquet of plastic calla lilies. During the services, Tangi had loved watching the small flames, imagining the warmth radiating from them and warming her heart. She always sat in the front pews, close enough to smell the burning candles mixed with the smell of soap that never seemed to leave the church.

Today, those candles were placed on both sides of the coffin. They flickered and danced as they always did, but this time offered no pull.

The funeral arrangements had been uncomplicated. Uncle Thomas—Papa's only brother—had paid for the coffin, food for the guests and anything else that needed paying for. Tangi spent the day before the funeral visiting one farm after the other, collecting sunflowers for decorating the church. She also created the flower arrangement for the coffin using wildflowers, ivy and twigs. The last one she would ever make her father.

The strong whiff of musk perfume wafted from Aunt Dabina in front of Tangi and hit Tangi's nostrils. She cleared her throat silently to stop from coughing. Funny that she still remembered her aunt's name. The last time she'd seen both her aunts, she'd been four years old. Papa had taken her to visit them in the city. They should have stayed a week, but the aunts had treated them like strangers and they had departed after just a day.

Now, here were her aunts at his funeral, flaunting black suits, sunglasses, and gaudy golden watches. Aunt Bini wore rings on all the fingers of her left hand. This brought to mind the ring hanging around Tangi's neck. Her mother's ring, made of the finest gold, unlike her aunts' jewelry.

They pretended to care about her Papa, but Tangi knew better. They didn't care; not about her father, and not about his children. Outside the church, Aunt Dabina had compared her and her sisters to mice that needed a good spray of pesticide. She spoke as if she wished Tangi and her sisters had died along with their father. It hurt Tangi deeply.

When Papa had been alive, only Uncle Thomas had visited them in their tiny mud hut, on Mr. Bunya's farmland where her father had been employed. Tangi loved Uncle Thomas. The wrinkles around his mouth spoke of a thousand smiles. His broad shoulders had carried her on so many piggyback rides. He'd often brought along a burlap sack filled with food.

Her father had earned so little money that most nights Tangi's stomach growled with hunger. Nona and Maria—fifteen and seventeen respectively—did chores now and again for Mrs. Bunya, the farmer's wife, to earn more money for food.

Tangi did help out as often as she could but wasn't able to do everything Nona and Maria did. Her right leg was much shorter than the other so she didn't have good balance when she walked or ran. Even standing for more than a few minutes caused pain in the foot and ankle of her shorter leg. Nona and Maria picked on her all the time about it, telling her she was a freak. But with her almond eyes, curly hair, and skin the color of coffee with a dash of milk, people often said that Tangi was the most beautiful of the three of them. Papa had always told her that she was teased because she was special, and one day she would be great. Since the first time he said it, Tangi hung on to that promise. The promise that one day, she would be better than all of them.

Aunt Dabina stepped into the front pew and sat down next to Nona and Maria. They both sat ramrod straight, unreadable expressions on their faces. Nona clutched a crumpled tissue and Maria blinked more than usual.

Tangi wished the three of them were close. A hug from them would have been comforting.

Uncle Thomas appeared, sitting down beside her. He was the only person she could trust. He squeezed her hand and she looked up. His thick, dark hair and moustache, and even darker eyes, shone with warmth and softness as always, but this time raw sadness also pierced through them.

Everyone had settled into their seats now. Not that the church was filled. In fact, only the first two pews were. A total of six family members occupied the first, and Mr. and Mrs. Bunya and two other people from the village sat in the second.

Pastor Markus, grey haired with a widow's peak, cleared his throat and moved to the pulpit. "Let's begin."

Tangi had known him all her life. It was strange; before today, she used to find the well worn leather-bound Bible ever present at his fingertips soothing.

Now there was nothing he could say to take away the pain.

He flipped the Bible open and the thin pages rustled as he leafed through it. "The Bible says the Lord is close to the brokenhearted; he rescues those whose spirits are crushed." He paused and glanced up at the congregation, giving the words time to sink in.

Tangi tried hard to believe what he said, longed for the words to wrap themselves around her heart like a bandage to stop the bleeding, but they bounced right off her.

Pastor Markus read three more verses about life and death and said something about Papa having found a new and better place to be.

"Instead of grieving, you should celebrate the life he had."

What life? Tangi wanted to ask. Exactly what about her Papa's life was worth celebrating? He'd lost her mother, had no money and most of his family had turned their backs on him.

Tangi peered at her aunts. Aunt Dabina's attention was on the cell phone in her lap. She punched the keys furiously and only looked up once or twice. Aunt Bini crossed and uncrossed her legs and sighed so loud, Uncle Thomas shot her an angry look.

Aunt Bini met his gaze and raised an eyebrow.

After forty minutes of preaching and reading the Bible, Pastor Markus closed it and a hymn was sung. Then he asked Papa's siblings to say a few words. Aunt Dabina dropped her cell phone into her bag and got up.

Tangi's heart rate quickened as her aunt approached the pulpit. Of everyone here, Dabina had something to say? Just the thought of having her near Papa's coffin made Tangi upset. She had no right to be here, and nor did Aunt Bini.

As far as she was concerned, Uncle Thomas was the only one who had the right to call himself Papa's sibling.

Aunt Dabina faced the congregation and shifted the rim of her black hat so her face was more visible. With her tiny chin and eyes that bulged out of her face, she resembled a bug. She dabbed her dry eyes with a new white handkerchief. "My brother was a great man." Her voice squeaked, like the mice she'd accused them of being. Then she regarded the coffin. "I loved him and will miss him very much."

Tangi couldn't bear to listen to her lies anymore so she sprang out of her seat and lunged for Aunt Dabina. "Liar!" she screamed. "You never cared when he was alive." She yanked and shoved her by the lapels, knocking her hat to the floor. There was the sound of tearing, but Tangi did not take notice. "You didn't even know him, witch!"

A shocked gasp.

Aunt Dabina pushed one of Tangi's hands off and grabbed at her collar. Tangi lifted her free hand to claw at her bug face.

"Why did you come? We don't want you here. My father should be here and you should be the one who's gone." The words tumbled out of Tangi's mouth without thought. The pain caused by her father no longer being there stabbed her insides. She wanted her aunt to feel it too.

Then Uncle Thomas took her in strong hands and pulled her away. She squirmed, broke free. Then she whirled around and ran down the aisle. Pain shot up her leg. She tripped, picked herself up again and burst out of the church door.

In the church courtyard, she collapsed at the damp base of a tree, hugging her knees to her chest. Hot tears spilled out of her eyes. She wept until the dam of her tears dried up and all she could do was hiccup.

In need of comfort, she reached up to touch her mother's ring that hung around her neck. It was gone. She patted her chest and searched the ground around her. Nothing. The sturdy string must have come untied when her aunt grabbed at her collar. Tangi pulled herself up from the ground and pressed her back against the cracked tree trunk to steady herself.

She let go of the tree and inched forward. The thought of losing the ring filled her with dread. When Papa had given it to her on her tenth birthday, she'd promised to take care of it.

Tangi stepped over a water puddle and limped to the church steps. She peeked through a slit in the door and ran her eyes down the aisle. No ring in sight. Perhaps she should go back inside. But Uncle Thomas stood at the pulpit. If she walked in now, everyone's attention would be on her.

Returning to the base of the tree, Tangi

closed her eyes. Then she remembered.

"If it ever gets lost, don't worry. It will find its way back to you," Papa had said as he'd pressed the ring into her hand.

She had nodded without understanding. Maybe now was the time to find out. But what if it never came back? She couldn't bear losing a piece of her mother. No, she would venture back in when the church was empty, before going to the cemetery.

Cemetery. The word vibrated in her mind and made her dizzy. The thought of her father being buried deep in the ground suffocated her so she pushed it out of her mind. She wouldn't think about it until she had to. For now she watched a robin pecking a nearby branch with no care in the world. If only she could turn into that bird.

Fifteen minutes later the door of the church swung open and Uncle Thomas walked out, his face etched with sorrow. He approached Tangi and pulled her up from the ground and into a hug.

"I'm sorry about your father, Tangi. I know today is hard for you." He stroked her hair.

She buried her head into his shoulder. He smelled of soap and dampness from the rain.

"I'm sorry, Uncle Thomas. I didn't mean to be rude in church." But that wasn't entirely true. She was not sorry for what she had done to Dabina. She deserved to be exposed for the fake that she was.

Uncle Thomas let her go but kept his hands on her shoulders. "Nobody is angry with you. You were upset."

She looked up at Uncle Thomas and blinked away the blurring in her eyes. "Uncle, what will happen to us now that Papa's gone?" Since Papa died, Mr. Bunya, the farmer, and his wife had allowed her and her sisters to stay with them until after the funeral. Tangi was sure that now they would be passed on to family. She prayed they didn't have to go and live with one of their aunts.

"Your father asked me to take care of you. You and your sisters are coming to live with me." He squeezed the bridge of his nose. "I always wanted to take care of all of you. Now that I can, he's no longer here."

"Thank you." She knew what he meant. For years Uncle Thomas had lived in Lonin, the capital city, where he'd worked as a taxi driver and earned very little.

Before Papa died, Uncle Thomas had started up a constructions business. The business was so successful that soon after, he'd bought a farm in a nearby village. There was talk of moving in with him, but it was delayed so that she and her sisters could finish their current school year.

"It would be nice to have you around. I'll send someone to pick you up in two days." Uncle Thomas cocked his head in the direction of the church. "Come back inside with me."

She followed him with no objection. Inside the church, she kept her eyes focused on the coffin, ignoring the invisible daggers from her aunts and sisters.

As Pastor Markus said a final prayer and all eyes closed, Tangi bent forward and scanned the ground for her mother's ring. No sign of it near the pulpit or under the pews.

All had been said in church so the funeral was brief. Tangi had been too drowsy to remember much of it. The only thing that would forever be engraved on her heart was her father's coffin being lowered into the ground, the smell of damp earth, and Uncle Thomas' firm hand around her shoulders as she wept.

That night, she fell asleep holding on to three small, clear, empty bottles Papa had given her shortly before he died.

That morning, her sisters had been at the village tap collecting water and Tangi had stayed back to care for him.

She'd been dabbing sweat off his forehead with one of his old shirts, when he'd reached under the blanket and pulled out the bottles.

His hands had trembled as he'd handed them to her. "These are for you," he'd whispered. "They're precious. When the time is right, you'll know why. Take very good care of them."

Tangi had nodded. There was no opportunity to ask questions; his eyes closed and never reopened. He'd left not only the hut silent, empty and cold, but also her world. As tears flooded her eyes, she'd buried her head into his chest and inhaled deeply, searched for his familiar smell. Instead of the scent he usually carried with him, all she could smell was the salty sweat he left behind after fighting so hard for his life.

She still had no idea what the bottles meant, but they were all she had left of him. That was reason enough to take care of them.

Chapter Two
Another Place

Tangi sat sandwiched between her two sisters on a tattered mattress in the back of an old roofless truck that smelled faintly of petrol. Two days after her father's funeral, Uncle Thomas had sent a trusted friend, Mr. Bolo, to fetch them and take them to his farm, which was about four hours away.

She watched the place she had spent her entire life diminishing behind them. When they drove past the cemetery, she blinked away tears.

Soon the village was as small as a grain of sand. Then it disappeared. Just like her father had.

"You're acting as if he was only your father," Nona said loud enough so the words didn't get carried away by the strong wind. "Crying won't bring him back. He's gone."

Tangi wiped her eyes. She had thought at least at this time they would put their differences aside and be a family.

She cast a glance at Maria, seventeen and the oldest of the three of them. Surely she would berate Nona for being so insensitive.

Not a chance. Maria shifted closer to Nona and they chatted in low voices, ignoring her.

Tangi wouldn't let it go. "I know he is gone, Nona. You don't need to remind me of that. But he's alive in my memories. He always will be."

Nona smirked. "So you had a stronger connection with him? Is that what you are trying to say?"

"I didn't say that." They always knew how to twist her words to suit them.

"You didn't have to. Just because you have a funny leg, you think you're special, don't you? Well, you're not. You're just weird."

Nona's words stung but Tangi wouldn't give her the satisfaction of seeing her hurt. She opened her mouth to say something but closed it again. What could she say?

Instead she folded her arms over her bent knees and rested her head on them.

As they rode on in silence, the air heated up and the wind blew stronger. Tangi prayed they would arrive soon, but it was still a long ride. She got tired of waiting and curled up in a corner of the mattress. She fell asleep soon after.

The truck was pulling into a petrol station when Tangi woke up. Nona and Maria lay sprawled on the mattress, both fast asleep. While a man in blue overalls tanked the truck, Mr. Bolo came to the back and handed her a small bottle of cold water.

"Thank you, sir." Tangi unscrewed the cap

and took a deep swallow, enjoyed the water cooling her mouth and throat.

Mr. Bolo climbed back into the truck and drove out of the petrol station.

Even though she was still thirsty, she knew Nona and Maria would be thirsty too. Pushing their earlier quarrel to the back of her mind, she touched Nona's arm.

Nona rubbed her eyes awake then Tangi handed her the bottle. Nona grabbed it without thanks, drank her fill, and then woke Maria for her share. Between them, they emptied the bottle.

Tangi gritted her teeth and looked away so they wouldn't see the anger and pain in her face. She could never get used to her sisters' dislike for her. But she did try to understand them.

Their mother, an alcoholic, had run away two years before Papa married Tangi's mother. They had never accepted either Tangi or her mother. If she too had been rejected by her mother in such a horrible way, maybe she would have turned out like them.

Half an hour later, the truck slowed down in front of a rusted wire gate. Beckoning from the other side was Uncle Thomas' farm. Dozens of cows, goats, and sheep grazed in the field around the compound, which was a group of huts and a small cement block building, surrounded by a fence made of long wooden poles to separate it from the farmland.

The driver climbed out long enough to push open the gate. Then they rode down a dry, dusty path toward the compound. The truck slowed down under a giant African Marula tree and the engine faded to a meaningless drone. Nona and Maria got up and climbed out of the truck themselves, while Mr. Bolo lifted Tangi from the truck and lowered her to the ground just as Uncle Thomas strode from the compound toward them.

"Hello, all of you. Welcome to your new home." His white teeth gleamed through his thick moustache.

Tangi smiled back, happy the ride had come to an end. "Hello, Uncle."

Uncle Thomas hugged each of them, handed Mr. Bolo a few notes, and lifted their single small fabric bag from the back. "Come on, girls, follow me."

On their way into the compound they passed two women who looked to be in their twenties. One towered over Uncle Thomas and had a horsey face that sported an angry-looking scar right in the middle of her pointed chin. Conversely, the other had a baby face, although she also sported an impressive double chin.

They both wore thin braids and scowls on their faces.

"This is Selma and Lisa." Uncle Thomas gestured at each of them in turn. "They take care of things around here. Whenever you need anything, just ask them."

Tangi extended her hand to Selma, the horsey woman. "Nice to meet you." The woman gave her hand a brief squeeze—her hand was rough like parchment paper—and dropped it almost immediately as if it were a piece of hot coal.

She refused to think much of it and shook Lisa's hand. Not quiet warm either, but at least she'd forced a smile.

"You must all be hungry. I'll put your bag inside your hut. Lisa and Selma have prepared some food for you, so go ahead and eat."

Tangi's stomach groaned in silent answer. Food would be nice.

They followed Lisa and Selma to an open kitchen area, separated from the rest of the compound by wooden posts positioned close to each other around it. A scrubbed wooden table stood on one side of the kitchen. Atop it was a large, square plastic bowl filled with plates, cups and spoons. A three legged black pot bubbled on an open fire in the middle of the kitchen.

Tangi and her sisters sat down at the table on the plastic chairs that framed the table.

Lisa poured drinking water from a bucket into metal cups and handed them to the three of them. Selma placed a big plate of *lisha*—a stiff porridge made from millet flour—in front of them, along with another one filled with rich meat stew. The rich meaty aroma wafted in the air and made Tangi's mouth water.

After serving the food, Lisa and Selma disappeared from the kitchen and left them alone to eat.

Uncle Thomas entered the kitchen five minutes later. "Everybody happy?"

Tangi nodded but didn't look up as she chewed her food, savoring every mouthful, and licked the stew from her lips. Too salty, but she didn't care. She and her sisters weren't used to having so much food around.

"I guess you are. I'm going to the shop. Get some rest."

Tangi lifted her eyes then. "We will, Uncle."

Maria stopped eating as well. "Do we all have to share a hut?"

Uncle Thomas stroked his moustache. "For now. Don't worry. It's big enough. I had it built just for you. I'll see you later." He strode from the kitchen.

Maria snorted when Uncle Thomas left them. "Perfect. I'm almost twenty and still have to share a hut with a twelve-year-old."

"Sucks, right?" Nona dipped lisha into the stew and lifted it to her mouth.

Tangi didn't understand why they had a problem with sharing the same hut. When their father was alive, all of them had lived and slept in a hut barely large enough for the four of them.

This hut was at least three times larger than that. It had two small, square windows, letting a stream of golden light enter. Three single beds with metal railings stood side by side on the cemented ground. On each bed lay a face cloth, a toothbrush, toothpaste, and a bar of soap.

Tangi closed her eyes as she sank into the mattress of the first bed she'd ever slept in. If anyone told her this was heaven, she probably would have believed them. No scratchy blankets and no waking up stiff from sleeping on the hard ground. She pushed aside the pain of the last few days and allowed the sweet smell of the freshly thatched roof to relax her.

Chapter Three
The Outcast

Tangi sat alone on the steps at the back of Muuli Village Primary School, away from all the laughter and the games at the front of the school. From this side, all she could see was the graveyard stretching out into the distance, surrounded by a rusted iron fence and dotted with dead trees and bushes.

She studied the different types of headstones—some weathered, some new—made of concrete, granite and marble. Dead flowers surrounded most of them.

She thought of the people buried under them. Someone, somewhere, had loved them just as she'd loved her father. She'd missed him so much since she moved to Uncle Thomas' farm. Right now she needed him more than ever.

Just as she was lifting a strawberry jam sandwich to her mouth, a black and white ball rolled to the back of the school and hit the fence. A boy with a shaved head appeared to fetch it without even paying her any notice.

Tangi bit into her bread and chewed without tasting it, the sweet aroma and taste of the jam just as distant from her as her classmates.

Two weeks after they arrived, she started attending the new school, ten minutes away from the farm. The village had no high school for Nona and Maria to attend, so in a few weeks they would leave for boarding school in a town six hours away.

On her first day, she had looked forward to making new friends, hoping some people out there would be nicer to her than her own sisters ever would be.

Although at her old school she hadn't had many friends, she hadn't minded too much. She'd had Papa to go home to. He took away the pain of being ignored all day. They read together, took long walks, making sure the crops grew all right, and she helped him take care of the baby animals, especially those neglected by their parents. She enjoyed stroking the head of a calf as she used a baby's bottle to feed it.

Without her father, Tangi had to face the world alone. The new school was supposed to be her new beginning.

But she had been ignored, and her high hopes had crumbled. The only thing her classmates seemed to notice was her short leg and limp. Whenever the teacher asked her to write something on the board, everyone's gazes dropped to her legs, and snickers and whispers filled the class room until Miss Lombe raised her hand and told them to keep quiet and pay attention. Sometimes they listened and sometimes they pretended not to hear her. After all, her voice was quiet and soft, which in a class of twenty-five pupils often worked against her.

Tangi liked Miss Lombe, who was easily the prettiest teacher in the school. She was petite and wore a cute braided bun, as if she carried a small basket on top of her head. She also wore a perfume that reminded Tangi of the smell of early spring when the flowers bloomed and shared their scent with the world.

One day last week, when the bell rang to signal break time and the other classmates had melted out of the class and into the school yard, Miss Lombe had stopped Tangi before she left the room.

"I know it's hard for you being new here. It's never easy being a new pupil." She placed her small hand on Tangi's shoulder. "I want you to know that we're pleased with you. You've adjusted well and your grades are impressive. Never mind what others think of you. One day, you'll be way ahead of them."

She meant well, but Tangi knew the reason the others acted the way they did had nothing to do with her being a new kid. At her old school, being new attracted popularity. New classmates often came equipped with new games and stories to share.

By the end of the second week, Tangi ended her pursuit of being liked. She stopped laughing at dry jokes just to fit in, stopped helping classmates when they struggled with their school work, and stopped asking to join in games at break times.

Instead, she decided she'd be her own friend. Besides, who needed them? Well, perhaps she did – but she'd never let them know. During breaks she retreated to the back of the school and sat on the steps, eating her food or reading one of the fairytale books she borrowed from the library. Her father used to read them to her all the time, and in her head, she often pretended to be one of the princesses she read about— beautiful, with perfect legs and married to a handsome prince.

It was a farfetched dream, she knew—but she would be more than the girl with the limp one day.

A voice pulled Tangi back to the present and she looked up surprised. "Can I sit with you?"

A girl of about her age stood in front of her. In one hand she held a red lunch box; in the other was a book.

Tangi thought she resembled some of the dolls she'd seen in shop windows the first day her father had taken her to the city.

The girl's face fell a fraction. "If that's all right, of course. I just thought you might need some company. I do. My name is Fye. I'm new in your class. I already know your name."

Tangi stopped staring and nodded, shifting

to create space for her. She clasped Fye's hand in a handshake. "Nice to meet you, Fye. I'm sure you heard a lot about me already. I'm the girl with the short leg." She hadn't meant to say that. It just spilled out. Everyone referred to her that way.

Fye grinned. "I don't know that name. I only know Tangi."

Tangi beamed. Someone saw her as a real person with feelings. "Thanks." What else could she say? When someone said something nice to her, it stuck. "But why did you choose to sit with me? It's more fun on the other side." She had to be sure Fye wasn't just there until the other pupils pulled her in.

"I needed a friend and you seemed nicest. I think you and I can have more fun than those fake people on the other side." Fye unclasped her lunch box and removed two slices of apple. She handed one to Tangi.

Tangi took it gratefully.

Fye's offering to her was more than just a slice of apple. She offered her friendship.

*

On Friday, Tangi jumped out of bed before the first cock crowed. Since she had met Fye, the dread of going to school had disappeared and given way to excitement. Despite the desperate attempts of other pupils to draw Fye away, her new friend had stayed put.

Tangi washed her face and put on her uniform—a white blouse and black skirt.

In the kitchen, her bread for school waited for her on the table on a plate, next to a basket filled with uncooked black eyed beans. She pushed it into a wrinkled plastic bag and put it into her school bag.

When she turned to leave the kitchen, she saw Uncle Thomas standing at the entrance between the two poles. He wore a grey suit and carried a shiny black bag.

"Morning, Uncle. Where are you going?"

Uncle Thomas stepped further into the kitchen, careful not to let the sand get onto his polished shoes.

"I'm going to the city for a few weeks. There have been a few complaints from the owners of one of the houses my company built. I need to go and see what can be done. There are also some other things I need to take care of."

Tangi frowned. "Is it very serious?"

"Nothing that can't be resolved in a few weeks. Don't bother yourself. You just concentrate on your school work." He pulled a few notes from his breast pocket and handed them to her. "Here; some of this is for your books; the rest is yours. Get yourself something nice."

Tangi wrapped her hands around the smooth crisp notes. Mostly, she bought books; the library often sold off some of its older, more worn copies.

Uncle Thomas looked at his watch. "I should go. I already talked to Nona and Maria. Do you want me to drop you off at school?"

"That would be nice."

Less than five minutes later, Tangi arrived at school. She got out of the car and Uncle Thomas waved and drove off in a cloud of dust.

Chapter Four
Cruel Surprise

Two days after Uncle Thomas left, something blunt poked Tangi in the chest. She opened her eyes to see Lisa, standing beside her bed, an oil lamp in her hand. In the dim light, her double chin jutted out even more.

"Get up," she hissed. "There's a lot of work to be done."

Tangi rubbed away the sleep from her eyes. She shook her head in confusion. "What do you mean?"

Lisa threw aside the blanket and goosebumps rose on Tangi's legs as the cold morning air assailed her. "Your uncle is not here to spoil you. Get dressed and go fetch water. Be back in time to help with breakfast." Lisa strode out of the hut.

Tangi stared after the trail of light from the lamp until it disappeared out of sight. Her head reeled with confusion. Was Lisa implying that she didn't do anything around the house? Even though Uncle Thomas had two housekeepers that did the housework, she still did her share. She washed her own clothes, washed the dishes, swept their hut and carried out other chores that didn't place too much strain on her leg. But never mind; one day couldn't possibly do that much harm.

Her eyes adjusted to the darkness. Lisa hadn't woken Nona and Maria. They continued sleeping, unaware of what had just happened. Not that they'd care.

Let them sleep, she thought, and heaved herself out of bed. Since Papa died, it hit her that people didn't live forever. She had relied so much on her father's love and care for her, like leaning on a strong, immovable tree trunk. Now she was afraid to depend on anyone, even Uncle Thomas. Being rejected at her new school also fueled her decision to learn to be strong for herself. She would prove to everyone she could do everything that they could. She wouldn't let her disability be an excuse, wouldn't give anyone reason to pity her. She'd get the water from the tap and learn to handle the pain in her leg.

Tangi pulled on her everyday dress that lay crumpled at the foot of the bed and went in search of a bucket. Just then a rooster crowed.

She found a bucket in the kitchen by the hearth. It rested on its side, knocked over by the chickens since they ran freely in the compound.

On her way out of the compound, she woke Jenga, Uncle Thomas' livestock shepherd dog, a smooth-haired fox terrier. Together they headed for the village tap. As they made their way down the path leading to the main gate, she was glad she'd brought the dog with her. With no lights in the village, who knew what the blanket of darkness hid?

The village tap was fifteen minutes from the farm, and Tangi had to return three times to collect enough water for both washing and cooking. By the third round, her arms ached from holding the bucket up on her head. Her foot and ankle throbbed with pain. None of her earlier confidence remained; now tears burned her eyes.

When she took the water to the kitchen, she found her sisters and the housekeepers sitting on plastic chairs around the table. She withdrew a chair of her own and joined them.

"What do you think you're doing?" Lisa's tone was sharp, clipped.

Tangi cringed. What did they want her to do now?

"The fire won't light itself. Go and collect firewood!"

Tangi bit her lip to stop it from trembling. Without saying a word, she limped out of the kitchen and into the field to collect firewood and some straw.

Back at the kitchen, she crouched down on the ground in front of the hearth and lit a handful of straw, which she poked under the firewood to help it catch on. Soon it caught and she blew on the flames to help it burn faster. Her eyes stung. Smoke plugged her nose and throat, and she coughed, gasping. Then, finally, yellow and orange flames flickered, sending sparks drifting upward.

Hesitantly, Tangi returned to her seat at the table. This time, no one said anything.

Lisa filled the black kettle with water and placed it over the open fire.

As they all waited in anticipation for the kettle to boil, Tangi eyed the half a loaf of bread and a jar of jam that sat on a plastic tray on the wooden table. Her stomach growled in reaction to what she saw.

Selma heard it and scowled.

When the tea was poured and the bread sliced, Tangi held out her plate, but Selma placed thick slices of bread in the plates of everyone else but hers. Then they all smeared their bread with jam and started to eat as if she wasn't even there. No bread remained for her, not even a crumb.

She gazed from the housekeepers to Nona and Maria. She couldn't understand what had happened. What had she done?

When Uncle Thomas had been here, the housekeepers had displayed no signs of holding anything against her. They had been distant when she arrived, sure, and she had never seen them smile. But they had treated all of them with indifference, Nona and Maria included. The sudden change stunned and confused her.

After a few minutes, Lisa stopped eating, picked up one slice of bread from her plate and passed it to Tangi.

Tangi reached for it gratefully but before her fingers could close on the bread, Selma snatched it.

"What do you think you're doing?" Selma glowered at Lisa, who shrank in her chair.

Tangi sat motionless in her chair, watching them, then shrugged. She pushed back her chair and shot out of it, wincing as the pain shot up her leg. She stomped out of the kitchen without looking back and went to their hut, where she stationed herself between their three beds and closed her eyes as confused thoughts whirled around in her head.

When she pulled herself together, she got dressed for school and left the compound. It was forty minutes before school started, but she didn't care. She headed for the village shop and bought herself some fried cakes and a can of lemonade.

Chapter Five
The Truth

Over the days that followed, Tangi forced herself to adapt to her new circumstances and obediently carried out the chores given to her by Lisa and Selma. The more she walked during the day, the more her foot and ankle throbbed when she went to bed at night.

Since she was never offered any breakfast, as soon as she brought the last bucket of water home, she simply got ready for school and bought something to eat from the village shop.

Going back home after school filled her with dread. She hated being surrounded by people who never talked to her unless ordering her to do something. She did everything—pounding millet into flour, cleaning the compound, washing all their clothes. And cooking food she didn't eat, unless she hid some for herself.

She became accustomed to the knot in her stomach that started forming halfway into the school day and tightened when the bell shrilled at the end of the school day.

"Ready to go?" Fye asked, approaching Tangi's desk.

Tangi and Fye had formed a routine that started with meeting at the school gate in the morning and ended with walking out of it together at the end of the day. Their first stop after school was Uncle Thomas' farm, where Tangi would fetch two buckets and they would then fill them at the tap. The water was used for cooking supper and washing the dishes. With Fye helping her, she was able to fetch more water.

"Yes." Tangi gathered her books and they left.

Forty minutes later, they had buckets filled with water balanced on their heads.

"Still okay?" Fye looked back at Tangi, who took small steps to prevent the water from sloshing out of the bucket as she limped.

"I can manage for five more minutes."

"Okay. Let me know when you need a rest." Fye tightened her grip on her own bucket and faced ahead again. "I still don't understand why your sisters can't fetch water as well."

"They know how to suck up to Selma and Lisa. They keep buying them things. I guess that does it."

"It's just horrible. I hope you tell your uncle as soon as he gets back."

"I'm definitely going to." Tangi repositioned the bucket on her head. Water gushed out in a small wave, drenching her school shirt. "Thanks for helping me, Fye."

"Don't worry about it. That's what friends are for."

*

Two weeks later, Tangi sat under an African Marula tree in the field, making sure the cattle stayed away from the crops, as she did every afternoon.

To while away the time, she was constructing a bouquet of flowers, made of white daisies, pepper green strands of grass, twigs and wire. She plucked, twisted and wrapped until she was satisfied. As she observed her creation and stroked a fragile petal between her thumb and forefinger, a tiny smile found its way through the uncertainty of the past weeks. But the glow she felt from creating something so beautiful wasn't warm enough to thaw the hard, slowly growing block of ice in her stomach.

Tangi placed the bouquet on a bed of grass next to her. She would create another one, she decided. She longed to feel happy again. But a nagging doubt in the pit of her stomach told her it might never happen. Fine, she thought. Somewhere close to happy should be fine.

She heaved herself off the ground to go on the search for more flowers. As she did, she spied a car pull up at the gate. Even if she was too far away and the sun too blinding, she knew it was Uncle's car. She shielded her eyes to block the sun and gazed into the distance. A man got out of the car to open the gate. It was him. Unable to repress her excitement, Tangi gave up on the cattle and bouquet making and limped as fast as she could toward the compound.

When she arrived, Uncle Thomas engulfed her in a hug. "It's so great to see you." The warmth of his smile echoed in his voice.

Tangi felt herself relax in his arms. Everything would be all right from now on. She would tell him everything. "I'm so glad you're back."

Together, they walked into the compound.

"Go find your sisters and come to my sitting room."

Uncle Thomas' room had a small sitting room attached to it. It was simple, with a fabric covered sofa, two chairs and a wooden coffee table.

Tangi found her sisters in their hut, braiding their hair. "Uncle's here. He wants us to go to his sitting room."

In the sitting room, Uncle Thomas handed Tangi, Nona, and Maria each a glossy plastic shopping bag. Tangi looked inside hers and pulled out a blue dress with tiny red flowers and a white lace collar. Nestled underneath the cotton fabric, she also found a pair of red leather sandals.

"This is beautiful. Thanks, Uncle." Tangi held the dress to her body and inhaled the clean scent that came attached to new clothes. A small thrill coursed through her. She couldn't wait to try it on. Now she had two church dresses. Just as well; her older one had seen better days.

Nona and Maria grumbled their unwilling thanks, and then left. They didn't seem very grateful, Tangi thought.

"It's great to see you girls. Was everything all right while I was gone?"

She pushed the dress back in the bag, avoiding his eyes. She knew she had to tell him, couldn't lie to him. But when she opened her mouth to speak, the words wouldn't come. Instead, when she looked up at him, tears welled up in her eyes and warped his face into a hazy blur.

Uncle rushed to her side. "Tangi, are you all right? Sit down." He guided her to the sofa and held her elbow as she sat down.

He pulled a chair to the sofa and dropped into it, facing her. Though her vision was fogged by tears, she could see his brow, furrowed with worry.

Uncle Thomas pulled a handkerchief out of his trouser pocket and handed it to her. "What's wrong? Did something happen? You can tell me anything."

Tangi knew she could, but for some reason, she was tongue-tied. Why couldn't she just tell him? A small, faint voice answered inside her head. *You're not a small girl anymore. You must fight your own battles. Show them how strong you can be on your own. Your uncle won't always be there.*

She wanted to ignore the voice, tell it to shut up, but there was some truth to what it said. She had vowed to herself that she would be strong on her own, that she would no longer rely on anyone, because they wouldn't always be there. What if she told him everything and he did nothing? Then she might end up having to suffer more.

She wiped her eyes dry and blew her nose. "My foot has been aching all day." It was true. In fact, she couldn't remember a day in the weeks Uncle Thomas had been away that she had no pain. "I don't feel too well."

Uncle Thomas looked down and examined her foot. "Should I give you something for the pain?"

Tangi nodded. Papa had never liked her to take painkillers unless absolutely necessary, but she had tried everything lately—massaging it like Papa used to do or dipping it in cool water for a few minutes before she went to bed. Nothing helped anymore.

"Good." Uncle patted her on the shoulder and got up. "I'll go to the shops to get you the painkiller and something nice to drink. I suggest you lie down for a while."

Tangi gazed at the sofa, and intense exhaustion washed over her. "Can I lie down here?" There seemed no better place that she'd rather spend the day; here, away from her sisters and the housekeepers.

"Sure." Uncle Thomas walked to the door. "I'll see you in a little while."

When the door closed, Tangi drew her legs up onto the sofa and lay down with a contented sigh. She fell asleep almost immediately.

Thirty minutes later, she was awoken by a rap at the door. Why would Uncle Thomas knock? "Come in." Her voice was drenched in sleep.

The door creaked open and Lisa came in, carrying a cup in one hand and what looked like a packet of painkillers in the other.

Tangi tensed up. She had hoped Uncle Thomas would bring the painkillers himself, not Lisa or Selma.

Without saying a word, Lisa placed the cup and packet of tablets on the coffee table.

Tangi couldn't help noticing that she didn't seem herself. Something about her — maybe the way she slouched or avoided her eyes — was new to Tangi. She also noticed the way Lisa dragged her feet as she walked to the door.

"L—Lisa?" Tangi swallowed. She hadn't meant to call her. The last thing she wanted was talk to her. But curiosity got the better of her.

Lisa stopped and turned.

Tangi cringed. She should have kept her mouth shut.

"What?" Lisa's voice was blunt. No sign of the edge Tangi had come to be familiar with in the past three weeks.

What had happened to break her spirit?

Tangi knew she had to say something now. "Are you okay?" Her voice shook.

For a moment their eyes met.

"I thought you...you don't look well." Watching her now, she really didn't. Her eyes were blank and underscored by dark shadows.

"My mother's very sick. She almost died last night." Lisa's voice broke.

"I'm sorry." Tangi meant it. She knew only too well how it felt to have a sick parent. She pushed aside the hate she had felt for Lisa and gazed at her with new eyes. "Will she be all right?"

Lisa's double chin wobbled. "I don't know."

A long silence followed. "Tangi, I know I have no right to ask you this after everything. Please don't report me. I need this job to help pay for her treatment. If your uncle finds out what we—"

"You did?"

Lisa's eyes slithered from Tangi's. "I need this job. Please forgive me."

Tangi sat up. Watching Lisa, the pain of the past weeks washed over her and brought with it the sweet taste of revenge.

But she couldn't enjoy it. If Lisa lost her job and her mother didn't get the treatment she needed, Tangi would feel partly responsible if she died.

"Why did you treat me so bad? What did I do to you and Selma?" Maybe, if she could understand them, she could forgive them.

Selma was the ring leader. Tangi had known it from the day Selma almost strangled Lisa for giving Tangi some bread.

"When you came here, it meant more work for us." Lisa paused. "I didn't want it to get this far. I told Selma a couple of times it was enough, but she was furious. She said if I betrayed her, she'd find a way to get me fired. I need this job."

"But why did you treat my sisters differently?"

"They promised to try and convince your uncle to increase our pay."

"They hate me," Tangi said, but hadn't meant to be heard.

Lisa perused Tangi's legs and looked back up at her. "They said you used your disability to get closer to your father."

Tangi's stomach twisted. They had no idea how hard it was to be her, how much she wished she could be like them. With two perfect legs. She wanted to reply to what Lisa had said, but didn't.

The silence was broken by Lisa's repeated plea. "Please don't tell your uncle." Guiltily, she glanced at the closed door, as if expecting someone to be hidden behind it, listening.

Much as Tangi wanted to continue despising

her, how could she? She too lived in fear of Selma.

"I won't."

After Lisa left the room, Tangi lay back on the sofa.

She was in a vise. Lisa had apologized, so she was going to keep her mouth shut. She wasn't sure if she had forgiven her, but it didn't matter for now. Lisa needed the job to keep her mother alive.

But Tangi knew she couldn't protect her without indirectly doing the same for Selma. She rubbed her eyes and groaned. She couldn't tell Uncle Thomas that Selma was the only one responsible. And if she did tell him, she knew Selma wouldn't go without a fight. She might not even hesitate to place all the blame on Lisa.

On the other hand, she thought, maybe she didn't need to tell Uncle Thomas anything. Things would be different now. She was protecting Lisa; Lisa had to protect her in return. Now that Lisa had more to lose, she might try harder. The worst was over.

The thought twirled around in her mind, relaxing her so much she fell asleep.

Chapter Six
Reaching Out

Uncle Thomas turned on the engine and Tangi waved. For two weeks he had been home, but now he was returning once more to the city.

In the car's backseat sat Nona and Maria. Uncle Thomas was dropping them off at boarding school. Neither of them looked up to wave goodbye to Tangi.

When they had driven off and the dust had settled, she walked back into the compound. She was left alone with Lisa and Selma, but it didn't get to her as much as it used to.

She relied on Lisa to shield her from Selma. She'd had another talk with her and she'd promised she would.

If only Tangi knew it wouldn't be for long.

*

The school day had ended and Tangi and Fye walked toward Uncle Thomas' farm to pick up the buckets of water. As soon as Uncle Thomas left yesterday, she had decided she would do the work Selma would demand of her before being asked.

As Tangi pushed open the rusted metal gate, she saw someone approaching them from the direction of the compound.

The person was Lisa. In her hand she held a small faux leather bag, colored with red and white stripes and decidedly worn out. She was hunched, as though the world was weighing heavily on her.

"Where's she going?" Fye wanted to know.

Good question.

"Where are you going?" Tangi asked. She injected a dose of lightness into her voice, but something didn't feel right.

Lisa slowed down. "My mother's condition has worsened. I'm going to take care of her."

Tangi's heart thudded inside her chest. "But...but you can't go." Even as she said the words, she knew she was being selfish. But she couldn't help it. "I can't stay here alone with Selma."

Lisa shook her head. "I need to be with my family. I have to go."

"What about your job? You need it to take better care of your mother."

Lisa's hard gaze wavered. "I'll come and talk to your uncle when he gets back." She hoisted the strap of her handbag higher on her shoulder and left.

*

Tangi told herself that Selma's problem was laziness. Surely if she did as much work as possible, she would be fine.

The morning after Lisa left, she woke up at the rooster's first crow before Selma had a chance to wake her.

By the time Selma was up, the water had been delivered, the fire lit, and Tangi had left the compound to meet Fye at the gate.

When she came back home, the sun had already gone down and Selma was nowhere to be found.

Just when Tangi thought maybe she'd gone out, she saw the glow of light forcing its way through the slit under the door of Selma's hut.

She tiptoed to her own hut. Without bothering to light her oil lamp, she changed out of her uniform into her sleeping dress and climbed under the blanket. If Selma thought she might go looking for food, she would be disappointed. She had already eaten at Fye's.

For a long while she was tense, expecting Selma to come in and demand where she'd been all day. But she didn't, and Tangi finally closed her eyes and slipped into a deep sleep.

The next day followed with the same success.

Then her luck ran out.

*

Tangi found it hard to get out of bed today. Much as she willed her eyes to open, they just remained shut. She wrapped her grey blanket tighter around her body, intending to snooze for just a few more minutes.

Then the sound of heavy footsteps ripped her out of sleep, and she jolted upright. Then, in a swift movement, she pulled her housedress over her head and smoothed it down her body.

"What are you still doing here?" Selma stood in the doorway, eyes sharp, hands on hips. "Getting lazy, are you?"

"Sorry, I ... I'll go now." Tangi tried to push past her, but Selma grabbed her tightly by the arm, her fingernails sinking into Tangi's flesh. "You're hurting me."

Selma held on a little longer, probably enjoying the look of agony on Tangi's face, before she let go.

Tangi spun away and headed for the kitchen to get the bucket.

When she arrived back from the tap, Selma was at the kitchen table thickly smearing a slice of bread with jam.

"What took you so long?"

"I didn't take longer than usual. If you're faster, why don't you do it yourself?" But Tangi mumbled these last words of defiance.

She stepped further into the kitchen and was just about to lift the bucket from her head when, to her horror, Selma leapt out of her chair and slapped her hard across the face.

Tangi gasped as the pain stabbed her cheek. The bucket slipped off her head and hit the ground, sending cold water splashing all over their feet. She gaped at the bucket and then back at Selma.

Selma pointed at the empty bucket on the ground between them, face contorted with rage. "Look what you did, you fool. Now pick it up and fetch more water."

Tangi bent down and got hold of the bucket handle. This was a fight she couldn't win.

*

The beatings got worse and more frequent. One week after the first time Selma slapped her, Tangi wondered if she should go on protecting Lisa. She wasn't even sure if she would be coming back to her job. She decided it was not worth it. She had suffered enough. It was time to think about herself.

Before she left for school, Tangi dug into her fabric bag, searching for a crumpled piece of paper with Uncle Thomas' phone number scribbled on it.

*

The bell went off to signal break time. Tangi and Fye left the classroom together and headed for the principal's office.

Tangi took a deep breath and knocked on the door. Last night she'd made a decision to tell someone apart from Fye about Selma.

"Come in," the principal called from the other side of the plain wooden door.

Fye touched Tangi's arm. "Do you want me to come in with you?"

"Yes, I'd like that." Tangi pushed the door open and walked into the tiny office. Light, buttery sunshine flowed through two windows, making the room feel more open, less claustrophobic. The wonderful scent of fresh air wafted in with it.

"What can I do for you two?" Mrs. Namula wore a suit, pants and a blazer the color of a beetle's shell. Her hair was pulled back into an afro puff.

Her kind tone took Tangi by surprise and sent her determination spiraling upward. Before today, she had been frightened of her. She resembled a Goliath with wide lips and large eyes.

"Go on." Fye nudged Tangi forward until the distance between her and the wooden desk was the length of a ruler.

Tangi ignored the wild mess of papers on the desk and unfolded the piece of paper. Her lips trembled. "Can you help me, please?"

"Sure. Is everything all right?"

Tangi handed her the note. "I need to talk to

my uncle. It's urgent. Can you call him for me?"

Mrs. Namula studied the note with a small frown. "Are you sure this is his number in Lonin?"

Tangi nodded, confused. It had to be. Uncle Thomas had given it to her before he left.

Mrs. Namula picked up the handset. "It looks rather short." But she dialed regardless and waited for the phone to ring, then shook her head and put the handset back in its cradle. Then, pursing her lips, she picked it up again. She redialed, held the handset to her ear and waited longer this time. Finally she hung up. "Are you sure this is the number your uncle wrote down for you?"

"Erm … yes. No. He told me the number and I wrote it down. It should be correct." Tangi wiped the palms of her hands on her skirt.

"Looks like you left out a number. It didn't even ring."

"Are you sure?" Tangi reached for the piece of paper. She and Fye moved their heads closer to study it, but it didn't tell Tangi anything. She had no idea how long a phone number was supposed to be.

"I'm afraid so. What you want to tell your uncle seems very urgent. Is it something I can help you out with?"

Tangi swallowed hard and looked at Fye.

"Tell her," Fye whispered.

"Fye, would you mind if I talk to Tangi

alone?" Mrs. Namula asked, glancing at Fye.

"No problem. I'll wait outside." Fye squeezed Tangi's hand and left.

"Take a seat, Tangi."

Tangi pulled out a chair and lowered herself into it.

"Is everything all right?" Mrs. Namula's eyebrows drew together. "If it's something serious, you should tell me."

And so, despite the woman's off-putting frog-like features, Tangi found herself telling her everything.

"And your uncle doesn't know any of this?"

"I couldn't tell him."

Mrs. Namula pushed her chair back and rose. "You shouldn't be going through this. Is this housekeeper at home now?"

"Yes. I think so."

"Is there anyone you could stay with until your uncle comes back?"

"I could stay with Fye, but Selma knows where she lives. She might come after me."

Mrs. Namula picked up her handbag and walked around the desk to where Tangi sat. She placed her hand on Tangi's shoulder. "How about you stay with me? Your uncle knows me. I don't think he would mind. I don't think you should go back to staying with Selma. I'll go there now to get some of your things. That is, only if you want to, of course."

"I'd like that very much. Thank you." Tangi

hadn't seen that offer coming but it was perfect. She would be safe.

The principal hoisted the handle of her handbag over her shoulder. "Don't worry about it. I'm happy you told me. Do you want to come with me to pick up your clothes?"

Tangi shook her head.

Just then the bell rang and break time ended.

"All right then. Go off to class, and come to my office after school."

When Tangi sat down for the next lesson, Fye turned to her. "I'm so glad you opened up to someone who can help you."

"Me too. It feels really great."

A long pause settled between them.

Tangi didn't think much of it. As the other classmates streamed into the class and took their seats, she leafed through her history textbook to page fifty-two, as the teacher had written on the blackboard.

But then the silence stretched too long. Even in between the scraping of chairs, backpacks being unzipped and pens being uncapped, she could hear it loud and clear. Then she noticed how rigidly Fye was sitting, her hands folded in her lap. She had not even opened her book.

Tangi sharpened both their pencils and put them down on the desk. "Wow, you look happy for me."

"I am."

"Then why do you look like you just saw a ghost?"

The corners of Fye's lips curled but her posture remained stiff. "I'm so happy for you. Especially now."

Tangi turned in her chair until she faced Fye. A ripple of fear now tainted her relief. "What do you mean by especially now?"

"I'm going away. My parents and I are moving to another place."

Tangi shot upright in her chair. "No! Why? When?"

"They should be waiting for me in the car outside right this minute. I just came today to say goodbye to you."

She couldn't. Not another person leaving her behind. Another person she cared about. "You can't go, Fye."

Fye wiped at her eyes. "I wish I could stay but…I've no choice. I'm not the one who made the decision."

Of course Fye hadn't made the decision; that came down to her parents.

It was Tangi's turn to be silent. How would she bear coming to school without Fye being there? They had spent so much time together, in school and out. But if Fye's parents wanted them to move, there was nothing she could do about it.

"I can't believe you're leaving. I'll miss you so much."

Fye grabbed Tangi's hands. Her eyes sparkled. "I'll miss you more. We just have to believe that we'll see each other again one day. I'll find a way to see you again. I have to go."

Fye and Tangi hugged tightly. Then Fye stood up and so did Tangi. She wanted to see her friend off.

Fye shook her head. "You don't have to come with. It will be too hard."

Tangi sank back down. Fye was right. She wouldn't want to make things harder. "Bye."

"Bye."

Fye weaved her way through the desks, talked to the teacher for a few minutes, then disappeared out the door.

Watching the window, Tangi waited for Fye to pass so she could wave one final time. But she didn't. How weird. No one could walk to the gate without passing that window.

Telling the teacher she needed the toilet, Tangi slipped out. She headed for the school gate, where she stood, staring. No Fye, no car, no one. She had disappeared as if into thin air.

*

"Are you ready to go?" Mrs. Namula walked up to Tangi. In addition to her purse, she carried Tangi's blue fabric bag.

Tangi nodded and smiled through the cobwebs of confusion Fye had left behind. "Yes, I am." She climbed into the car.

Mrs. Namula placed both hands on the steering wheel as she drove. "I confronted Selma. She denied everything, but I can tell a liar when I see one. It's one of the skills one learns from being a principal."

Of course Selma would lie.

"What did she say when you told her I'll be staying with you?"

"She didn't seem to care. I'm sure your uncle will deal with the situation when he comes back. How evil can someone be to hurt a child?"

Tangi shrugged. At least she couldn't hurt her anymore.

Chapter Seven
Sweet Relief

Tangi and Mrs. Namula stood inside the compound, in front of a small white brick house, similar to the one on Uncle Thomas' farm but bigger.

Mrs. Namula hugged her twin daughters—both were six years old, with chubby cheeks and big brown eyes—and her face softened. When the girls had had enough and squirmed from her hug, she turned them to face Tangi. "This is Sima and Malena. Girls, this is Tangi. She'll be staying with us for a while. Make her feel at home, okay?"

Two pairs of eyes studied Tangi's face, like roommates trying to decide whether to take her in or not. Then their faces brightened. "Can she stay in our room?" one of them asked.

Tangi gazed from one girl to the other. She had never met twins this identical. How did people ever tell them apart? Then she got it. One of them had pierced ears and the other didn't.

"No, Sima. I want our guest to rest. I don't want you two disturbing her. Is that clear?" Mrs. Namula looked at one of the girls, expecting an answer.

"Yes, Mummy." The twins nodded and a moment later they skipped off to play.

"Let me show you your room, Tangi."

They entered the brick house and walked down a short corridor past two closed doors. Then Mrs. Namula stopped at the third and pushed it open. "This is where you'll be sleeping. Rest for a while. Dinner will be ready soon. I'll send the girls to come and get you."

The room was small but cozy, with medium-sized windows and a thin brown carpet. She had never been inside a carpeted room before. She removed her shoes and stepped inside. Then she placed her bag on the single wooden chair and sat down on the bed, running her fingers over the brown duvet. It felt so soft against the palm of her hand, almost like a petal. She picked up one of the pillows, held it against her chest and studied the room further. A solid pine wood wardrobe stood against the wall in front of her. It was too big; she only had three dresses and two sets of uniforms. Did she even need to unpack? After all, who knew how long her stay would be.

She shut her eyes for a moment, reveling in the peaceful and comfortable atmosphere. The ripple of children's laughter drifted through the open window and broke the silence. But laughter was good. It reminded her she was in a good place.

Suddenly, exhaustion swept through her. She changed out of her uniform and curled up on the bed. Moments later sleep enveloped her.

A soft voice coming from the door woke her up. One of the twins—she wasn't sure which—peered through a crack in the door. "Dinner is ready. We're eating potatoes and chicken stew. I helped with the cooking." The little girl's face was a picture of satisfaction.

"Hmmm...that's nice." Tangi sat up in bed and tried to focus her eyes. She was torn; she would love to sleep some more, but she was also hungry. "I can't wait to taste it."

She heaved herself off the bed and followed the girl and the rich aroma of the stew.

As they walked, the little girl reached up for her hand and held on to it. "Can I plait your hair after dinner? Mummy taught us how to do it."

Tangi touched her hair, her plaits a tangled mess. She used to plait her hair herself—two cornrows, one on each side of her head. But with all the work on Uncle Thomas' farm, she had not had time and so had neglected them.

Tangi, Mrs. Namula, the twins, and the nanny—an older woman with hair so grey it was almost white—had dinner together in a closed kitchen as big as the room she was occupying. Tangi had only ever seen an open kitchen with a hearth. This kitchen was modern and had a gas stove and a fridge. Most people in the village cooked their food on an open fire and dried some types of food instead of freezing it. Even if someone found a way to get a fridge, they still had to think about getting a generator since there was no access to electricity.

*

During dinner the twins chirped about their day at school. Then their conversations changed to the presents their father would bring along when he came home.

"I'm getting a bride doll." One of the twins licked stew off her spoon and looked excitedly at Tangi.

"I'm getting a book on different types of insects." The other twin's eyes danced.

"Do you have a daddy, Tangi?" Sima, the twin with the pierced ears, asked.

Tangi stiffened at the question. Papa was dead, but she didn't feel quite ready to let him go. Saying it would make it too real.

"Let Tangi eat her food, girls." Mrs. Namula gave Tangi an apologetic look, rescuing her from the difficult questions.

After dinner, she pulled her aside. "My daughters are at a very talkative age. I hope they didn't say anything to upset you."

"Not at all. They're sweet."

"I'm glad to hear that. I want you to feel comfortable here."

She really used to be afraid of this woman?

This woman who looked at her with so much kindness? "I am. I am comfortable here. Thank you so much." Tangi smiled. She really was very grateful to her for everything. "Is there anything I can do to help around the house?"

"No. Why don't you go ahead and do your homework? You don't need to do anything. You're our guest."

Tangi went to her room, unpacked her books and got started on her math homework. It only took her forty-five minutes.

"Can we come and do your hair now?"

The twins stood at the door with pleading eyes. Sima sucked her thumb as her sister spoke.

Great timing, Tangi thought. "Of course. Come in."

The girls hopped onto her bed. Within ten minutes, they had unraveled her hair. An hour later, her scalp felt tight from the fresh cornrows.

"You can look in the mirror now." Malena reached for a small square mirror and handed it to Tangi. "I told you we're good."

Tangi gazed into the mirror and turned her head from side to side. She looked really good.

She dropped the mirror on the bed and hugged them both. In the arms of the little girls, she felt more love than she had felt in a long time. "Thank you."

Chapter Eight
Dream And Reality

Except for occasionally scraping chairs and low murmurs, the class was quiet. Miss Lombe cast a glance at her watch, timing the math exam.

Math wasn't easy for most of the kids in Tangi's class, and it was obvious. As she surveyed the room, she noticed that some nibbled on pen caps or stared into space.

Relief washed over her. At least she had studied for the exam. The principal encouraged her to spend as much time as she needed on her school work. And it wasn't like she had friends or anything to occupy her spare time with.

Tangi turned her attention to the paper in front of her. She had answered almost every question. She reread the questions and answers as carefully as she could.

When she had reached the fifth question, a knock came from the door, then Mrs. Namula walked in.

All heads looked up. A welcome distraction for the bored pupils.

Mrs. Namula regarded Tangi briefly, and

then exchanged a few hushed words with Miss Lombe.

After she left, Miss Lombe tapped at her black leather watch. "Time's up! Pens down. Please hand in your exam papers."

The classroom burst with life as pupils scrambled from their desks or begged in whispers for last minute answers from their friends.

Tangi's delight at having completed the exam was sprinkled with sadness at not having a friend to whisper to. She missed Fye every day she came to school and had to endure a whole day without her being there.

No one else seemed to miss her much. Life went on. The desk that had belonged to her was now occupied by a pimply girl who was always secretly chewing gum.

Tangi slipped out of her desk and handed the two pages to Miss Lombe.

"Stay here for a moment, Tangi. I have a message for you." Miss Lombe continued receiving papers, stacking them on top of each other on her desk.

Tangi stepped aside to let the others walk past.

Once the room was empty, Miss Lombe turned to her. "Sorry to keep you waiting, Tangi. Mrs. Namula wanted to speak to you. It sounded important."

"Okay, I'll go to the office." Tangi headed to the door.

"You'll have to do so after break, I'm afraid. She's out at the moment."

When break time came to an end, Tangi knocked on Mrs. Namula's door and was asked to enter.

"I found your uncle's phone number." Mrs. Namula closed a grey folder. "I talked to him this morning. I told him what had happened, but I thought you might want to talk to him too."

"Yes, I'd like to."

Mrs. Namula dialed the number and handed the phone to Tangi. The phone rang three times, then she heard his voice.

"Hello, my dear girl." His warm and comforting voice brought a lump to her throat.

"Hello, Uncle."

"Tell me, is it true what your principal told me?"

Tangi nodded as she grabbed the phone with both hands.

"Tangi, are you there?"

"Yes, Uncle, it's true. It's been going on since the first time you left."

"Why didn't you tell me?" His voice dropped in volume.

"I don't know," she mumbled. She couldn't tell him she was protecting Lisa.

"I want you to stay with Mrs. Namula until I return. I'll be there in three days."

"Okay."

"In the meantime, I don't want you worrying

about a thing. I'll sort it all out when I come home."

That night, Tangi didn't fall asleep easily. When she did, she stumbled into a weird dream.

*

The dream started with Tangi arriving at Uncle Thomas' compound from school. The pit of her stomach felt hollow and empty from hunger.

Hoping to find some food, she headed for the kitchen, but all she found there were dirty plates strewn across the table. Two hens pecked at the dry remains on the plates.

She sank down into one of the dusty plastic chairs.

What had she expected? Selma never left her any food. It was up to her to fend for herself. But how? The money Uncle Thomas had left her was gone.

She stared at the empty chipped plate in front of her. Then a thought hit her. The storage hut. Why hadn't she thought of that before? It had never been an option because as soon as Uncle Thomas left, Selma usually locked it.

Tangi pushed herself out of the chair and walked out of the kitchen. Maybe she'd forgotten to lock it today. With every drag of her feet on the dry ground, she hoped and prayed that was the case. It was.

The shackle of the solid brass padlock hung

through a metal loop attached to the small wooden door, detached from the body.

This might be the only chance she'd ever get. She would not waste it.

She slipped into the hut, which was stocked high with all kinds of food. No time to be choosey, Tangi thought, and grabbed anything within her reach—half a loaf of bread, dried dates, and a can of Vienna Sausages.

When she was back in her hut, every piece of sausage and every crumb seemed to melt on her tongue. She inhaled the meaty smell of the sausages. Why had she taken only one can? She was tempted to go to the hut again but she stopped herself. This time she might not be so lucky.

She finished eating the bread and sausages and hid the empty can and the knife she'd used to open it under her bed. Then she moved on to the dates, closing her eyes to better enjoy the sweetness. Then she opened her eyes again and almost choked. Selma hovered over her, hands on hips, eyes slitted.

"Did you think you could just sneak around stealing food and not get caught?" she snarled and lifted her hand, about to strike.

Tangi choked down her food. She wasn't going to let her beat her again. Not this time. Not ever again. She ducked the blow, shot up from the bed and dashed out of the hut and out into the field with Selma close at her heels.

She ran-limped faster than she'd ever run in her life. Small thorns pierced her bare feet like needles, but she kept right on going.

Selma soon gave up and returned to the compound. Maybe the thorns had gotten to her.

Tangi slowed down, bent over, and put her hands on her knees. She struggled to calm her breathing and moved on to her favorite tree: the one she sat under when she watched the animals. She sat down and dropped her head on her bent knees. It began drizzling, which quickly turned to a hard shower, hurling down dime-sized droplets.

She lifted herself up off the ground and roamed around the field. Should she go back inside and face Selma or should she stay and get drenched? She decided to stay.

Before long, she was soaked. Even though her clothes hung heavy with moisture, her braids stuck in wet slicks against her neck, and water dripped into her eyes and mouth, she didn't care. Returning to the compound wasn't an option. Staggering across the field to different, perhaps better, shelter, mud squished between her toes.

A male voice came out of nowhere. "Slow down, Tangi."

Tangi slowed her walk and looked around her. No one there. Was she going crazy?

"You're not crazy. I am real." Whoever it was had read her mind. "I'm here. Look in the ditch in front of you."

She dropped her gaze and moved toward a ditch filled with dirty rain water. She looked inside, took in the muddy water, like coffee mixed with milk. Then she stepped back and shook her head. This was ridiculous. Turning, she resolved to return to her search. The rain had now quickened and raindrops tap danced all over her head and shoulders. A shiver rippled through her and she hugged her arms to herself.

"Don't go. I'm here to help you. You deserve more than this world will ever offer you."

Tangi stopped midstride and turned. As she walked back to the ditch, a little laugh escaped her lips. She reminded herself of Sarah, the crazy woman of the village, talking to herself, hearing things no one else heard.

But what did she have to lose? She would take another look, and if she still saw nothing, she'd leave without turning back.

She bent lower at the waist and peered into the ditch.

All of a sudden, the ditch filled with crystal clear water.

She jumped away, her heart pounding wildly, and then moved closer again.

Then the rain stopped. Sunrays slanted through the dark clouds and the air was suddenly heavy with the scent of roses.

When the water reached the rim, the ditch transformed into a pond. The crystal water shimmered. The mud had disappeared and the green of the leaves seemed more vivid. No sign at all that it had rained just a few seconds ago.

The reflection of a handsome man's face stared up at her—short, curly hair, big brown eyes, and the whitest teeth she had ever seen. He seemed to be somewhere in his twenties.

"Hi, Tangi, I'm Daryle, the prince of Rosevine. I didn't mean to scare you. I came to show you a way out of this world."

"This world? A prince?"

"That's not important right now. There's something I need to tell you urgently."

Tangi kneeled in front of the ditch turned pond. A lot of weird things had already happened. She might as well listen to what the man had to say. "All right."

"The reason you're being treated so badly is because you don't belong in Mimbeye. As long as you're there, you'll experience pain. If you want to escape it, you should come home where you belong."

"I don't understand. What are you talking about?"

"Your mother also used to be treated as an outsider when she lived in that world. Your father's relatives abandoned him because of her. She didn't belong there either. Everyone felt it."

Tangi inched closer to the edge of the pond. "You knew my mother?"

"Not personally, but she was one of us.

There's so much I want to tell you about her, but now is not the right time. I've come to tell you how you can escape." He paused. "If you want to."

A pebble dropped into the water, and the ripples distorted his face and his voice. Then the surface of the water smoothed again.

"If you really want to leave that world, you're always welcome to come home to Rosevine."

"I've never heard of it. Where is it?"

"It's hard to describe. Somewhere no one can access normally, and we can't force you to come here."

"How do I get there?" The words rolled off her tongue before she had a chance to think them.

"Do you still have the bottles your father left you?"

Chills ran down Tangi's spine. "Who exactly are you? And how do you know about the bottles?"

"I don't mean to scare you." He paused once more before continuing, "I'll tell you how, one day, when you understand everything. I hope you still have the bottles. You can't escape without them."

"I hid them. You know what they're for?"

"Yes, I do. They're your key out of there. They're no longer empty."

Tangi tilted her head and narrowed her eyes.

"I don't understand."

"All the tears you've cried since your father died are now in those bottles. When it's time for you to leave, you'll come and pour two drops of those tears into this ditch. It will turn into a pond, the way it did now. You'll dive in and resurface in Rosevine."

"How's that possible?"

"Anything is possible. You just have to believe."

"You mean that? All I have to do is what you said, and I'll end up in your world?"

"Not quite," Daryle said. "When your father died, he left your uncle the responsibility of looking after you. Even if you have the bottles, they will not open until your uncle lets you go."

"How do I do that? There's no way he'll believe all this."

"Don't worry. You'll get a little help. I hope you come to Rosevine. Our beautiful land is disappearing. As your mother's only child, only you can save it. You'll love it here, I promise. It's far from the place it once used to be, but there's still some beauty left. Bye for now." And then, with those words, Daryle's image disappeared.

The pond became a ditch again. Overhead, the sky blanketed with dark clouds, and it once more began to rain. This time it rained harder.

Tangi closed her eyes, willing the pond to return.

When she opened them, she found herself

staring up at the ceiling of her room in Mrs. Namula's house. It had all been a dream, a dream that had felt more real than anything she had ever seen or experienced in her whole life.

Despite the confusion, a warm glow radiated inside her body. If Daryle was right, she was going to be someone great after all.

Chapter Nine
Fruitless Search

Saturday afternoon, Tangi sat in the field with Mrs. Namula's twins, showing them how to make sunflower bouquets.

One of the twins, Sima, reached out and handed her one of the flowers she'd picked. "This one smiled the brightest."

Tangi took the flower from her, wrapping her fingers around the cool stem. "I can see that. You seem to know where to find the most beautiful sunflowers." Tangi lifted her gaze and watched the other pink clad twin, Malena, walking among the sea of sunflowers, searching for the ones most deserving to be put into a bouquet. She moved from one to the next, gazed down and shook her head. Picky little girl. "Why don't you help Malena find them?"

Sima nodded and ran off to accomplish her mission.

For a moment, Tangi gazed after her. Then her gaze was averted by movement. From a distance, she saw Mrs. Namula in front of the compound shaking a man's hand. Her heart began to thump with excitement. Uncle Thomas was back.

She gathered the bouquet the girls had already finished and jerked to her feet.

"Sima, Malena, time to go. Come and meet my uncle."

The twins' eyes brightened as they always did when someone came to visit. They held hands as they followed Tangi.

When they arrived at the compound, Uncle Thomas engulfed Tangi in a hug.

"I'm so sorry." He rested his bearded chin on top of her head. "For everything."

Tangi held on to him, closed her eyes. All would be fine now. "It's all right, Uncle."

He broke the embrace and looked her straight in the eye. "If anything like this ever happens again, promise you'll tell me."

"I promise." But it would not happen again, she knew; she was not going to stay long enough for that. She hoped the dream she'd had would come true. Since talking to Daryle, she hadn't stopped thinking about it. Now that Uncle Thomas had arrived, she would be able to find out if the bottles really had filled. Then she would know it was more than a dream.

*

Tangi and Uncle Thomas arrived on his farm and found no sign of Selma. In fact, it seemed as if no one had been on the compound for a long while; the hearth was dead, the chickens were roaming about, and the plates were dry and dirty.

She must have left the day Mrs. Namula showed up to confront her.

On one hand, Tangi was glad she never had to see her again, but on the other, she would have liked to see how Uncle Thomas dealt with her.

"What a coward." Anger contorted Uncle Thomas' face. "Anyone who hurts a child has to be one. I won't let her get away with this. I know where her parents live. She has to be there."

Tangi had more urgent things to think about rather than stand there thinking about Selma. She had to find the bottles.

She left Uncle Thomas in the kitchen and went to the back of her hut. She slipped behind a familiar shrub and dropped to her knees. Then she bent forward and swept aside a few twigs and leaves. The soil she had used to cover the hole was not as smooth as she had left it when she checked three weeks ago.

She pushed her hand through the soil as far as she could. Nothing. She pulled it out again and frantically started to turn the soil with both hands.

She kept digging, her mind a mixture of hope and fear. The sand caught between her fingers and stuck to her palms, but she didn't feel the smooth, hard surface of the bottles. There was only an empty hole.

Tangi collapsed on the ground. Her dream would remain a dream after all.

She sat there, head buried in her dirty hands. Why would someone be interested in empty bottles? It all didn't make sense.

But then, what if the person who had found them, not knowing their worth, threw them away? She couldn't bear the thought.

One thing was for sure. She had to do everything to find those bottles as soon as possible.

Tangi got up and went to the hut Selma and Lisa had shared. It was smaller than her own, and had one small window instead of two. The scent of the coconut lotion Selma had liked to wear hung in the air. She wrinkled her nose. It smelled to her like rotten coconuts.

She pulled her attention from the smell and started searching under the two single beds. She crawled all the way underneath and used her hands, running her palms over the ground and even raking her fingers through the soil. In the end she found a box of matches, a small comb, and a two-sided mirror. Nothing else.

Then she started to doubt her memory.

What if she had buried the bottles in a different place? The burial had been hurried so that she was not discovered.

But that couldn't be possible. They had been

there when she checked three weeks ago. She hadn't dug them up, but she'd inserted her hand into the soil until her fingers had touched the hard glass.

A quick and disturbing thought flashed through her mind. What if Nona and Maria had seen her hide them? They would take the bottles for the simple reason that they meant something to her. Meant enough for her to hide them.

*

Tangi and Uncle Thomas spent the rest of the day settling in and cleaning up the mess Selma had left behind. Uncle Thomas told Tangi to rest and let him do the work, but she insisted on helping. It wasn't as if he was forcing her, like Selma used to. She chose to do it, and she could choose which work she could handle and which not. Working also kept her mind from obsessing about the bottles.

While he raked the kitchen area, straightened the wooden posts surrounding the compound, and collected enough firewood to last a week, Tangi unpacked the bags of food Uncle had brought and put it away in the storage hut, which Selma had completely emptied. She also did other minimal chores, like scratching dry remains from the plates and placing them in a stack on the table or scooping ashes from the hearth with a shovel.

Uncle Thomas drove to the village tap and came back with two ten-liter plastic barrels, with screw-on lids, filled with water. He carried one to the kitchen and the other to the corner behind Tangi's hut where she washed herself.

"I don't want you to ever carry anything so heavy that it hurts your leg, so no more carrying water. From now on, I want to be home for longer stretches of time. If you need anything, anything at all, you let me know. I'll always be here for you."

"Thanks, Uncle." Tangi felt a twinge of disappointment. He was so good to her and she would soon leave him. It was going to be hard to say goodbye. But leaving also meant he would not have to constantly worry about her or put his work on hold just to spend more time at home babysitting her.

He patted her shoulder and headed for his room to unpack. "It's been a long day. You should get some rest. Then we can eat some of that food your principal gave us."

"I'll do that. You should rest too, Uncle, after your long journey and all the work."

He stopped and turned around. "Don't worry about me. It's you I'm worried about. How's your leg, by the way? Any pain?"

Tangi looked down at her legs. "No, I haven't had much pain in the last week."

"I'm glad to hear that. But I'm taking you to the city when I go back so you can see a doctor for some tests." He walked into the brick house, and a moment later his door closed.

Instead of going to her hut, Tangi remained in the kitchen and filled a bowl with water and soap. She settled down at the table and began to wash the plates, enjoying the feel of the soapsuds between her fingers.

*

After supper, Uncle Thomas told Tangi stories about the city. She listened absent-mindedly until he went silent. Then she looked up at him.

"Uncle, when are Nona and Maria coming home?"

"You miss them already?"

She might as well lie. What else could she say? No? "Yes." Being with them was never fun. All they did was make her feel bad about herself. What reason did she have to miss them?

"Then I have good news for you. They'll be here tomorrow afternoon."

She sat bolt upright, a flicker of hope building up inside her chest. "Really? How long will they be staying for?"

"A week. Enough time for all of you girls to catch up."

No, Tangi thought. Enough time for her to search through their things.

*

Tangi drifted in and out of sleep all night. When the rooster finally crowed, she leapt out of her bed. Of course, it was way too early; Nona and Maria would not be home for hours yet.

Lunch time came and went. Still no sign of them.

Fine, she could wait. She didn't want to but she didn't have a choice.

Maybe she'd read a book. Yes, the collection of fairytales Uncle Thomas had brought her.

She flopped back onto the bed and opened the glossy hardcover. She read the first two short stories, and then the drone of a car caught her attention. Tangi slipped her feet into her plastic flip-flops and limped outside.

Outside, Nona and Maria climbed out of a minibus, and Uncle Thomas hugged them both.

They both wore long, tiny braids hanging down their backs. Nona wore tight jeans and Maria a mini skirt that Uncle Thomas kept eyeing with a look of disapproval. They also wore heavy makeup. If Tangi had met them somewhere else, it would have taken her a moment before she recognized them.

Tangi stepped forward. She really wasn't happy to see them, but was sure the feeling was mutual. In spite of this, she still hugged both of them briefly. Their eyes widened, and they shared a perplexed look. Tangi ignored this. She wanted to prove she was no longer intimidated by them.

If they had her bottles, she was determined to face them boldly. The secret of Rosevine strengthened her. She knew something they didn't. Something that was all hers. Unless she didn't find those bottles.

Back inside their hut, Tangi watched them unpack some of their things and made an attempt at conversation. "How's boarding school?"

They ignored her and didn't even look up. She shifted on her bed. They didn't want to talk to her? She couldn't care less. But she needed something from them. Getting closer to them— or at least pretending to be— could help, she thought. "Did you make many friends?"

Nona glared at her, lips thin with irritation. "Don't you have anything better to do, Limpy?"

Tangi squared her shoulders. "I just wanted to—"

"Don't!" Maria snapped. "It's bad enough having to share a hut with you."

Tangi nodded and hauled herself off the bed, the bedsprings sighing with relief as she rid them of her weight. Who needed them anyway? She didn't. And besides, hopefully she'd soon be gone so she'd never have to see them again.

She would find those bottles. She just needed to get to their things.

Tangi walked out of the hut, taking her book with her. She sat down on a chair next to the door and continued to read, ignoring the whispers drifting from the hut.

Fifteen minutes later, Nona and Maria left the hut, no longer wearing the clothes they had arrived in. They now wore matching black shorts and white T-shirts. They had, however, added more makeup.

"Tell Uncle we're going out. We won't be back by supper," Maria said over her shoulder as she passed.

Nona and Maria had probably gone to the *Music Box*, a shop in the village center that always brimmed with music and teenagers who attended boarding school in the same town as they did. Tangi had never been inside but she often passed it on her excursions elsewhere.

She waited a while longer before reentering the hut, making sure they didn't come back for something or other. Then she slipped inside, stomach clenched with nerves.

First she pulled Nona's bag from underneath her bed and unzipped it, letting out a zing. It was filled with lots of shiny and sparkly clothes. They didn't have a cupboard in the hut so they had only unpacked their toiletries and other small things.

Tangi removed all the clothes and gently shook out each piece over Nona's bed. She had to be careful so the bottles didn't fall out and break. With each piece of clothing that had no bottle inside it, her throat seemed to close up. Nothing she found concealed her bottles, and her throat only closed further and further.

Next, she moved on to Maria's things. But she still didn't find anything.

Tangi pushed Maria's bag back to its original place, pushed herself up to a standing position and went to sink down on her own bed. Her chin dipped to her chest.

If they didn't have the bottles, who did? The dog? Jenga constantly dug things up and played with them. Some of those things often ended up in the field and there was no guarantee they would be seen again.

Tangi rolled onto her stomach, arms covering her head. Should she give up? Resign herself to remaining in this world?

Who even knew if Daryle had not been a figment of her imagination? What if Rosevine didn't really exist? Maybe she had been so upset and had made it all up so she could feel better. But there had to be a reason why Papa left her the bottles.

She left the hut and went to pass on her sisters' message. Then she went into the field, searched for the ditch. It was in the same place as in her dream, only without water. She kneeled on the ground next to it and sat there until the sun lowered beyond the horizon and the warmth of the day faded. Then she went back to the compound to help prepare supper.

*

Tangi sat at the back of their hut, polishing her school shoes, when she heard Uncle Thomas' voice, taut with anger.

"You will not leave this house again without asking for my permission, in person."

Tangi shuddered inside. She had never heard him so angry before. He always talked to her in a gentle voice. But she didn't blame him. It was late morning and she hadn't yet seen Nona and Maria. They hadn't come home last night.

"And if you do go out, you will be back in time for supper. I will not tolerate this kind of behavior in my house. Is that clear?"

"Yes, Uncle. We're sorry." Maria's voice trembled.

Nona's voice followed, equally soft and muffled.

"You better be." Anger still dripped from Uncle Thomas' voice. "If this is the type of behavior that being at boarding school teaches you, I'll make sure you don't go next year."

There was a long pause, then the sound of heavy footsteps that grew fainter with each second. She guessed Uncle Thomas had walked off.

A minute later, Nona and Maria stepped inside the hut.

Tangi put down the shoe and sat motionless, listening.

"Talk about bad timing." Nona's voice was a hush but Tangi could hear every word drifting out of the window. "You have a date. There's no way you can go out again tonight, especially not after supper. What will you do now?"

"I can't believe this," Maria said, her voice trembling with rage. "I've had a crush on Daniel since the day we moved here. Now he finally notices me, and Uncle is treating us like children. I can't deal with this." From the creak of the bedsprings, Tangi knew Maria had sat down on her bed.

"But we can't get into trouble again, Maria. You heard what Uncle said. One wrong move and our freedom is gone. When we're at boarding school, at least we can do what we want. We can't afford to lose that."

"I don't care. He's not my father," Maria raged, and Tangi cringed.

How dare she say that? He had done so much for them. If not for him, they would be staying with one of their mean aunts right now.

"I'm not going to let a few stupid rules stand in my way. I'm meeting Daniel tonight. As for Uncle...." Maria paused. "He doesn't have to know."

"What if she finds out?"

"Don't worry about Limpy. She's too stupid to notice anything."

Tangi clenched her fists. The urge to jump up, burst into the hut to lash at them was overwhelming, but she suppressed it.

She listened as Maria shifted the conversation from her to what she would be wearing to her date that night.

*

Late at night, when the compound was silent and only the chickens clucked occasionally, Maria slipped out of her bed and dressed in the dark.

Tangi pretended to be fast asleep.

"Have fun," Nona whispered. "I'll make sure Uncle doesn't find out. But don't forget one thing."

"What?" Maria asked.

"You owe me."

"I know that. Bye, sis."

Maria exited the hut and left for her date.

Tangi and Nona fell asleep.

Soon after the rooster crowed, Maria reentered the hut, undressed, and crawled into her bed as if she'd been there the whole night.

Chapter Ten
Now Or Never

Nona and Maria were due back at boarding school tomorrow. Yesterday, Tangi once again ransacked their bags – but with no luck.

She went to bed racking her brain for what to do next. She couldn't give up without knowing the truth. The truth about who she really was.

She had only slept for about an hour when something jerked her awake. Glancing toward Nona and Maria's beds, she gasped.

A small light floated above Maria's bed, piercing the darkness.

Tangi squinted to get a better focus. The light was in the shape of a bottle, as small as the ones that belonged to her. She became instantly wide awake.

The bottle was glowing and Maria was awake, sighing as she twirled it from side to side.

The only time Tangi could get the bottles back was now. Tomorrow would be too late. But Maria would never give it up that easily, so Tangi watched her for a long time, thinking of a plan.

Maria twirled the bottle in the air until it seemed she got bored. Then she tucked it under her pillow and went to sleep.

Careful not to make a sound, Tangi climbed out of bed, letting the moonlight lead her. She pushed her hand under the pillow and, holding her breath, reached in further until her fingers felt the bottle's smooth surface. Then the blood rushed from her face.

Maria was glaring at her with burning eyes. "What exactly do you think you're doing?"

"I … umm." Tangi withdrew her hand. "A while ago I lost three small bottles. I … I saw you holding one of them."

"What the hell are you talking about?"

Tangi tilted her chin up and pinned her with a cool stare. "You saw me hide the bottles behind the hut and took them. I want them back."

Maria wrapped her arms around her pillow and squeezed it to herself. "You don't know what you're talking about. Now go away and let me sleep."

"I want my bottles. Right now," Tangi said between clenched teeth.

"Or what, Limpy?"

Tangi clenched and unclenched her fists as anger surged through her. This was her moment. She had to finally stand up for herself. "Even if you think I'm too stupid, I still know that you snuck out to meet a boy the day after you arrived. I also know that you didn't get back until morning."

Maria sat up in her bed and gazed at Tangi, speechless. Nona, who was awake by now too, also sat watching.

"I know everything, and if you don't give me back my bottles, I'll pass on that information to Uncle first thing in the morning."

There was a long pause.

This was great. For the first time, she was actually standing up to her sisters. "Or maybe I could just wake him now and tell him. You choose."

Tangi took a step toward the door.

Maria jumped out of bed and grabbed her arm. "Don't do it. I'll give you your stupid bottles. I don't know what you want them for anyway. All they do is glow in the dark. They won't even open."

"It doesn't matter. They're mine, and you had no right to take them."

Maria strode over to her bed and reached into her pillow. She removed all three bottles and placed them in Tangi's hands.

Tangi wrapped her fingers around them and exhaled. She felt almost dizzy with exhilaration. "Another thing," she said.

"What more do you want?"

"Don't ever call me Limpy again. I have a name and you know it."

"Fine." The words dripped with hate or

something close to it.

Tangi went back to her bed. No feeling could compare to the sense of victorious elation currently pounding through her.

The next thing was to try opening the bottles. In the dream, Daryle had said they wouldn't open until she got Uncle Thomas' permission to leave. Was that true? Was *any* of it true?

Holding up one of the bottles, Tangi tried turning the cap. It wouldn't budge. She tried harder. Still nothing. This was one further sign that her dream had been real.

Though she couldn't open the bottle, it was nice to watch it glow in the dark. Her tears inside it, if that was the liquid it contained, were clear and bright like liquid diamond.

Now Tangi understood. Even if the bottles couldn't be opened by Maria, the mysterious liquid inside had kept her from throwing them away. She closed her eyes, said a silent thank you, then tucked the bottles under her pillow and laid her head down.

Believing the impossible seemed to be getting easier now. There was something special about these bottles, something mysterious. Now she just needed to convince Uncle Thomas; then she'd be gone.

She couldn't sleep, her whole body filled with tremendous anticipation that kept her a-wake into the early hours of the morning. Her eyes finally fell shut just as the sun came up.

When she woke up, Nona and Maria had already left. She didn't even have a chance to see them for the last time. She shrugged. They hadn't been close, anyway. They probably wouldn't even miss her.

Tangi reached under her pillow to check on the bottles. They were still there.

Just like every morning, she brushed her teeth and had breakfast with Uncle Thomas, then went back to her hut and took the bottles.

Chapter Eleven
Number Thirteen

As Tangi stood in front of Uncle's door, about to knock, she felt her courage drain. Her hand dropped back at her side. This was crazy.

How would he ever believe a dream had led her to believe she could escape to some strange land? She had been a bit skeptical too. Until Maria handed her the bottles and they really were filled.

Not telling him wasn't an option, since his permission was necessary for everything to work. But it wasn't something to just spring on someone. She needed to think about this a little more.

*

Tangi sat on her bed with her hands folded in her lap, mustering up her courage. There was no easy way for her to tell Uncle Thomas. It would be like telling him she'd seen a ghost. But he had to know. And the sooner, the better.

"I'll see you later, Tangi." Uncle Thomas' voice drifted into the hut from outside. "I'm going to milk the cows."

When Uncle Thomas was not home, a boy from a neighboring farm usually milked the cows. Tangi had only seen it being delivered on the first day of Uncle Thomas' first trip, though. The rest of the time, Selma got to it first.

Tangi stepped into the doorway. "I'll come with you." She walked out of the hut to join him.

Uncle Thomas handed her one of the empty pails he was carrying. "It's nice of you to join me. Cows are not the best company."

Tangi felt a little pang. If only he knew why she chose to come along.

Uncle Thomas continued talking as they walked side by side. He told her about the approaching harvest, two goats that went missing yesterday, a calf shunned by its mother, and other issues that faced farmers.

She responded here and there, though her attention was lax. Her mind was focused on the painful knot in her stomach.

When they arrived at the kraal, she put down her pail and fetched the milking stool from the corner. Uncle Thomas sat down and with the wet cloth he had brought along, wiped the teats of the cow he would be milking.

"You're rather quiet, Tangi." He placed one of the empty pails firmly between his knees and started to milk the cow.

"There's something I want to talk to you about."

"Sure, what is it?"

"I … I, well, this will sound weird. I don't know how to tell you…."

He stopped what he was doing and looked up. "What is it?"

"I'm leaving." The words came out quickly, before she could change her mind. Then relief flooded her body. The hard part was over.

Uncle Thomas' eyes widened and his moustache seemed to droop. He shook his head. "What do you mean?"

"I'm going away, far away."

He wiped his hands with the wet cloth and stood up. He placed his hands on her shoulders. "Tell me what's going on. Where is all this coming from?"

She told him everything—the dream, Daryle, the tears, and Rosevine.

When she finished, Uncle sunk back down on the stool, lips pursed.

The longer Tangi waited for him to respond, the more slippery the palms of her hands became.

Finally he cleared his throat. "Tangi, you can't do something just because someone told it to you in a dream. How do you know it's even true?"

"I wouldn't have believed it, but I found the bottles. Just as Daryle had said, they are filled with tears. My tears."

"How can you be certain they are tears?"

"You're right. I don't know for sure, but whatever is inside is something special. The liquid glows in the dark."

Uncle Thomas stood. He picked up his pail, which had less than a liter of milk inside. "Let's go home. We need to talk about this some more."

Tangi didn't answer. She picked up her own pail and followed him.

When they arrived, he poured the milk into a jar. Then he pulled out a chair for each of them.

"I know you believe that what you saw in your dream is real, but people dream all kinds of strange things. It doesn't mean they are true."

"I know. I've dreamt a lot of dreams before. But this one is different. It meant something. I was confused at first too, but my father left me the bottles for a reason. Now I know what that reason is."

He reached for her hand. "You've gone through so much, my dear girl. You're just a little confused."

"I'm not confused." She spoke with firmness. "Let me prove it to you." She got up from her chair, left the kitchen and returned with one of the bottles.

She cupped her hands around the bottle, leaving a small opening. The tears in the bottle glowed in the semidarkness created by her palms. She moved closer to Uncle Thomas so he could look.

He didn't resist. When he looked up again, his face was still masked with questions. He still wasn't convinced. "This doesn't prove anything. Please understand, it was just a dream."

Tangi sighed. Trying to make him understand was proving to be impossible. But Daryle had said nothing was impossible. "It wasn't just a dream. I believe it, everything." She wrapped her hand around the cool bottle, squeezed it. "I wish you would too."

"I'm sorry. You're only twelve. Please understand that I can't let you leave. Your father wanted me to look after you. I can't let you go to a place I don't even know."

Tangi nodded. She understood his position but nothing had changed. Somehow, someway, she'd find a way to get him to see it too. The answer would come to her, just like Daryle had said.

*

Cautiously, Uncle Thomas kept a watchful eye on Tangi. He also made sure to spend more time with her, just sitting and talking. They talked about mundane things, but it was almost as if he feared she might be going crazy and he was trying to keep her sane.

Tangi, however, was alert for any sign that showed her the way to make him believe her. For a whole week, every night when she went to bed, she waited patiently for Daryle to show up in her dreams again, but he didn't, and the bottles still wouldn't open. Several times each day, she visited the ditch, looking for signs or answers.

Despite her search for the truth, life went on as usual. She and Uncle Thomas had found a routine. He did most of the chores in the compound, and she helped him out in every way she could—feeding the chickens, milking the cows, cooking and washing up. Anything she could do while sitting down.

Days fleeted by and the cold knot in her stomach hardened. Fear grew inside of her; fear that Uncle Thomas would never believe her and the bottles would stay closed, trapping her freedom inside forever.

Soon, she could not take it any longer. She had to discuss things with him again. Early one morning, she knocked on his bedroom door.

"Come in."

His face brightened when he saw her. "I was just about to come and wake you to congratulate you on your special day."

Tangi stared at him, baffled. What did he mean, her special day?

He crossed the room and hugged her, sending her mind reeling with confusion.

"I don't understand. Did I do something?"

"You don't know what today is? You forgot your thirteenth birthday?"

Tangi tried to picture the date in her mind. October twenty-fourth. It really was her birthday. "This is weird. I've never forgotten before."

"I think we should celebrate, and I have a great idea. You and I are going to Lorimi for the afternoon."

Lorimi was the nearest modern town from their village, but not near enough for one to walk to.

"We'll go there," Uncle Thomas continued, "and we'll buy you a new uniform and a few other pieces of clothing and shoes of your choice."

Tangi flinched. School was scheduled to start in only a week, and she had hoped to be away by then. She never thought she'd go back.

"Thanks, Uncle," she said halfheartedly.

"No problem. You deserve it. Now go and get ready. We'll leave in about an hour."

Tangi went to wash herself and get dressed. Uncle Thomas was making an effort to cheer her up. She decided to make an effort and pretend she was having fun.

Just as she slipped her feet into her flip flops, Uncle Thomas knocked on her door.

"I brought you this." He handed her a brown envelope. A look of sadness passed over his features. "Your father told me to give it to you on your thirteenth birthday."

When he left the room, Tangi sat down on the bed, holding it to her chest. Her heart wrenched with pain. Papa had thought of her birthday. It meant everything.

Brushing away the tears, she opened the envelope. Inside were two folded letters, neatly lined in her father's cursive. She began to read the first one.

My darling daughter,

If you're reading this, it means I'm gone. I'm so sorry for leaving you so soon. I wish I could be there to watch you grow into a beautiful woman just like your mother was. You're special, Tangi. I'm writing this letter to tell you just how much.

By now you've probably found out about Rosevine. I don't know how you were told, but you should believe every word. You belong in Rosevine, the place your mother came from. I know it might be hard to grasp, but it is the truth. Unfortunately, I was not allowed to tell you anything before you turned thirteen.

Before I left you, I asked your Uncle Thomas to take care of you because he loves you like his own daughter. I know he will find it hard to understand that you have to leave. That's the reason why I have written a separate letter for him, which you should also find in this envelope. In it, I have explained everything to him.

My princess, I wish you a better life than I could ever offer you. You deserve so much more.

Happy birthday. Never forget that I love you very much.

Papa

Tangi read the letter three times. Her hands shook so much she could barely hold it. She would never have believed that the answer she had waited for, for so long, was supposed to come from her father. Now Uncle Thomas would have no choice but to believe her.

The other letter really *was* addressed to Uncle Thomas. Without reading it, she picked it up and took it to him. She found him outside, washing his car's side mirrors.

"Papa asked me to give you this." She handed it to him.

His eyebrows lifted in surprise. "Really?" He placed the cloth on top of the car, unfolded it.

The longer he read, the more his posture drooped.

"You were right," he finally said. He folded it and put it in his breast pocket. "Sorry I didn't believe you."

Now that everything had worked out, she didn't know what else to say? It broke her heart seeing him look so defeated. She kissed him on the cheek. "Don't worry about it. It's hard for me to believe too."

She walked back into the compound and went into her hut. One last test. To see if the bottles would open.

The first cap she turned gave in with the slightest bit of pressure. She stared at the open bottle, speechless.

Just to make sure, she unscrewed the other

two bottles. No resistance at all. Daryle had been right.

Tangi decided to take up Uncle Thomas' offer to go to Lorimi, even though she would not need any clothes. After all, she was not taking anything with her.

After a tour of the small town, they had lunch at a restaurant called Juicy Pies. Tangi ordered a chicken pie. The name of the resaurant did the food justice, but she couldn't enoy it fully.

Uncle Thomas didn't say much and he looked so sad.

She hated leaving this way, but it also comforted her to know that without her there, he could focus on his business. He wouldn't have to rush back from the city when Tangi was not all right. Between her and her sisters, she was the one who required more care.

He did talk a bit more on their drive back home without turning to look at her. "When do you leave?"

She was excited and wanted to leave for Rosevine as soon as possible, but she owed him to stay one more night. To eat supper together for the last time and talk as they usually did afterwards. "Tomorrow morning."

"I'll miss you, Tangi."

Tangi touched his shoulder, memorizing the cottony feel of his checked shirt. "I'll miss you too, Uncle. I'll never forget everything you did for me."

"You're my brother's child. That makes you my child too."

"But you didn't have to let us come and stay."

"It's what you do for family you love."

*

When Tangi woke up, the sun had already risen and light bathed the room in faint golden light.

She tore a page from one of her exercise books, a book she'd never use again. Then she sat down to write a letter.

Dear Nona and Maria,
I know we don't have the same mother, but I have always seen you as my sisters. With me out of your lives, maybe you'll be happier. I'm writing this letter to tell you that I forgive you for everything.
Goodbye.
Tangi

Tangi found Uncle Thomas slicing a loaf of bread in the kitchen as a kettle boiled over the open fire.

"Did you have a good night's sleep?" He asked without looking up.

Tangi grinned. "I did."

Uncle Thomas placed the cut slices on two

plates and removed the kettle from the fire. "That's good. You hungry? I thought we could have breakfast together for the last time ... before you go."

"Sure, that would be nice." She pulled out a chair.

"So, tell me." He sat down. "Tell me again how you'll enter Rosevine."

She poured hot water into their cups. "I'm supposed to pour a few teardrops into the ditch. If everything goes well, it should fill up with water and turn into a pond. Just like it did in my dream."

"Then you have to dive into the pond?" He bit into a slice of bread and pretended their conversation was about something as normal as what they'd eaten for supper.

"That's what Daryle said."

"What if it doesn't work?" Hints of worry laced his words.

"If it doesn't, I'll climb right out. I can swim, remember?"

"Am I allowed to come and see you off?"

Tangi was touched. "Yes. I would like that so much."

"In that case, we better get going then."

Tangi returned to her hut for the last time. Instead of packing like most did when embarking on a journey, she just sat on her bed, letting it all sink in.

She had endured a lot while living on this

farm, but a part of her would miss being here. She would miss this hut, the smell of the thatched roof after the rain. Not long ago, this hut had been the only place she could find peace, and only in the dead of night. When everyone who had the power to hurt her was asleep, the hut had been her haven.

Enough thinking about the past. She stood up and pulled the bottles from the pillow, ready to go.

She stepped outside and Uncle Thomas reached out for her hand, and they left the compound together.

When they arrived at the ditch, he turned her to face him. "Can you promise me something?"

"I hope so." Tangi had no idea she would be able to keep promises all the way to Rosevine, a place out of this world. But he needed a little bit of assurance that everything would be all right. She would leave him with what she could.

He squeezed her hand. "When you get to Rosevine, find out if it's at all possible for you to come back and visit. I'm not ready to say goodbye forever."

Tangi swallowed hard. "Me neither." She meant it. He was the one person she would truly miss. "When I get there, I'll find out. I promise."

He hugged her for a long time. Then he let go and kissed her on the forehead.

"Goodbye, Uncle."

She removed one bottle from a small plastic

bag and unscrewed the cap. Then, stepping nearer to the ditch, she poured in the tears dropwise: one, two, three, four.

Just like in the dream, everything changed. The ditch transformed into a pond so beautiful it was hard to believe it was real.

Tangi beamed, so happy that Daryle had been right.

Uncle Thomas' face was a picture of disbelief. "I can't believe this."

"It's amazing, I know. Uncle, I have to go."

"Okay." His voice was stronger now. What he just saw must have reassured him that all the other promises of her happiness would also come true. That she would be all right.

She kissed his stubbly cheek, wrapped her fingers tightly around the plastic bag, and slid down in the water until completely submerged.

Chapter Twelve
Desert Heat

Tangi opened her eyes. Harsh sunlight blinded her. She snapped them shut again.

Carefully, opening her eyes by fractions, she let herself grow accustomed to the light.

She was lying on desert sand and her three bottles of tears lay next to her. She picked them up and got to her feet. Something was different. She tried to pinpoint it, then she got it. She didn't tip to the right as she used to when she stood. She lifted her right leg and studied it. It looked just like her left one, just as long. She lowered it down to compare some more. This couldn't be. Her face split into a huge grin.

She danced around in the sand, giggling and twirling until the contents of her head swam. If only Nona and Maria could see her now. If everyone could see her. No one would ever call her Limpy again.

She walked around, testing her brand new leg. Not even a hint of a limp. She would be happy here, in Rosevine. But this couldn't possibly be Rosevine. This was a desert.

Panic replaced her feelings of excitement.

Where was she and where was Daryle?

What if something had gone wrong and she had somehow gotten lost? Icy fear twisted around her heart. What would she do now?

But standing in one place wasn't going to help, so she picked a direction and set off.

Even if her legs were now the same length, it wasn't easy to walk when her feet sank into the soft, hot sand. But she wouldn't give up. She picked up pace, and then started to run. No pain. No tripping. No limping.

When she was too tired, she slowed to a walk, and then walked until she no longer could. A stitch pierced her side and she needed something to drink. If Daryle didn't show up, how would she survive in a desert without water or food?

She squinted into the distance—the heat making everything swim—and saw, not too far away, a hut made out of sand. The grains of sand hung unsupported in midair. Even stranger, Tangi could see through them, as if peering through a lace curtain. Like the ones she saw at Mrs. Namula's house.

She rushed to the hut, feeling the weird urge to limp because she'd been doing it her whole life.

When she reached the hut, she stepped inside. The temperature here was a great contrast to outside—cool and refreshing. Almost as if a gentle breeze surrounded her. After the burning heat, it felt great to be cooled down.

She pulled her attention away from the temperature and took a look around. A pitcher of water and a basket of fruits—apples, bananas, and grapes—stood on the ground, on top of a woven mat.

Tangi sat in the cool sand and eyed the picnic. She needed it. She didn't care who'd left it.

She raised the pitcher to her mouth and closed her eyes as cool water touched her lips and slid down her throat. Next she picked an apple from the basket. She'd never seen apples as large. They also shone as if they had just been polished.

The apple tasted of vanilla. She savored the sweet nectar until she reached the core. Even if it was big and she was full, her mouth still craved more. She reached for another and ate it slower this time, licking the juice off her fingers. Being full didn't stop her from also reaching for a red grape, popped it into her mouth. It had no seeds and tasted like honey with a hint of ginger spice. Strange, but very delicious.

But she couldn't stay. She had to continue.

Tangi stepped out of the hut. Less than a minute later, a swish came from behind her. She spun around and stared, amazed, as the hut crumbled into a mound of plain sand.

Someone must have left it just for her. Who? Could it be Daryle? Maybe he'd hear her if she spoke. "Daryle, are you there?"

"Yes, I'm here." Daryle's voice came out of nowhere. "You didn't have to leave the spot you landed on. I would have found you."

Tangi whirled around but didn't see anyone. "Where are you?"

"You won't be able to see me yet. Just follow my instructions so you can come to Rosevine."

She sighed and relaxed. It didn't matter that she couldn't see him. He had come to get her, hadn't left her stranded. "What do you want me to do next?"

"Look for a rainbow and walk toward it. Everything will be easy after that."

Tangi turned in a half circle, gazing into the empty distance, then spotted it. An arc of color shimmering in the light.

But as she approached the colors faded until they disappeared. A stone wall appeared in the rainbow's place. It had no beginning or end and was too high for her to see the other side. The closer she came to it, the cooler the sand beneath her feet got.

But there was no gate. How was she supposed to pass?

Then Daryle spoke again. "Touch it."

Tangi reached forward and tapped it with a fingertip. As if reacting to her touch, part of the wall disappeared and a beautiful golden gate appeared, wrapped in ruby red rose vines. Instead of a door handle, it had a golden metal rose with a diamond in the center. The word Rosevine floated in the air above the gate, it too adorned with matching roses.

Wow! She stared, tongue-tied. "What do I do now, Daryle?" It was a struggle to find the words.

"Touch the diamond too. And welcome to Rosevine, Tangi. I'll see you later."

"Where are you going?"

No answer. He was gone.

She reached out and pressed the cool, glinting diamond and the gate swung open.

Nothing could compare to the splendor before her. Stretched out in front of her was a path of seashells, strewn with multi-colored petals, the colors of the rainbow she had just seen. Tall rose trees framed both sides of the path. Rose trees? Everything seemed to be possible in this place.

Cupping her mouth with both hands, she giggled. Then she stretched out her arms as if she had wings, and shouted, "I'm free!"

Inhaling the delicious scent of the roses, Tangi walked through the gate and along the path. Petals showered her, feather-light and cool on her skin. She felt herself change. She had no idea how it happened, but something was definitely shifting inside of her, making her feel different. Her clothes also felt too tight on her.

Suddenly, the gate she'd just walked through disappeared.

A tingle of excitement went down her spine. She felt warm and safe, like being wrapped in a warm blanket on a cold night.

A faint sound made her stop. Birds sang a gentle song, and the rustle of leaves joined the lullaby. Butterflies of red, gold, and blue appeared and danced in the air as rose petals joined them. She gazed up at the sky—filled with clouds that looked like white cotton—and closed her eyes. Rose petals fell on her face and to the ground.

When she opened her eyes again, the shorts and T-shirt she had been wearing had changed into a swinging brown dress with light golden sleeves and hem. On her feet were matching chocolate brown sandals. Then the birds stopped singing. Apart from the soft rustle of the leaves, no other sound filled the air. The butterflies also flew away as if they'd just been sent to meet and dress her.

Tangi walked on down the path and came across a lake with two flamingos gliding on its surface. She kneeled on the bottle green grass and bent forward, reaching out to dip her hand into the water, and then jumped back when she caught her reflection.

She took a deep breath and looked into the lake again. Her fingers touched first her hair, then her face. The girl staring up at her from the lake looked different, older. "How can this happen? How did I grow up so fast?" She had to be at least twenty years old.

"It took you a number of years to get here, Tangi," a voice answered from behind.

She startled, turned.

A little man with a much darker complexion than hers came to stand next to her. On his head he wore a hat adorned with a peacock feather.

The man removed his hat, bowed, and then plopped it back on his shiny, balding head. "It's a pleasure to finally meet you. I'm Joe, the caretaker of Rosevine. I'm here to welcome you."

Tangi stood up, brushed the grass off her dress, and bent down to shake Joe's small hand.

"Come with me."

He led the way in a different direction from the one Tangi had been headed before. She picked up pace so they could walk side by side. For a small man, he walked rather fast.

"How do you find Rosevine so far?"

"It's amazing. I love it here."

"Not nearly as beautiful as it once was. The splendor is vanishing fast. Some places are hardly recognizable anymore." He turned to look at her. "We hope you'll agree to save it."

"What do you mean? How will I be able to save a land?" And besides, it didn't really look as though it needed saving.

"You'll find out soon enough, my dear."

She didn't want to wait. "What would I have to do? Is it difficult?"

Joe chuckled and folded his hands behind his

back. "Only you will be able to decide that. All I can say is that it would involve your tears and the prince."

Tangi slowed her walk and stared at her empty hands. The tears. They were gone. "I lost the bottles. I was holding them when I walked through the gate. I don't know what happened to them."

"Don't worry about it. Your tears are safe. Now, we'll go to my house, then I'll answer more of your questions."

*

Joe and Tangi arrived at a place where hill houses lined a shimmering river in neat rows. The houses had small doors and windows and well-tended gardens around each of them, where the people of Rosevine grew fruits, vegetables, and different varieties of flowers—daisies, forget-me-nots, tulips, marigolds, so many more. They all looked like happy homes, but something was missing.

"Where is everyone?"

"Oh, they're all at the HOC."

"The HOC?"

"The Hall of Celebration."

"There's a celebration?"

"A very important one."

Joe opened the door of his own hill house. Like all the others, it was adorned with precious stones and had a golden handle.

"Welcome to our humble home, Tangi." He held the door for her to enter.

Our. That must mean he was married.

The house was cozy and pretty, with wooden furniture and a marble fireplace in the small sitting room. From inside, hill houses didn't look much different from the houses she'd seen when her father had taken her to the nearest city just to have a look. Sometimes she had gotten the chance to take a little peek through a window. Inside they looked just like Joe's home, with armchairs and rugs and pictures on the walls.

"Come along."

They walked through the sitting room. On the walls were pictures of Joe with a bride on his arm. Tangi was not close enough to see her face, but she did see that she was very pretty and had a nice smile. She opened her mouth to ask him about his wife and whether they had children, but closed it again. They had just met; she didn't want to pry.

Joe led her to the kitchen.

She sat down on a chair by the table and watched him make tea.

"This is lovely. I've never seen hill houses before."

"Thank you for the compliment. All the houses in Rosevine are identical. The only ones different are those of the royal families. They get to live in castles on top of hills instead of inside them." He carried a large, steaming mug to her.

Tangi took the mug from his hands. "Thank you."

He sat and poured himself some tea, into a smaller mug. "Now, let me explain a few things to you. How about we start with how you grew up so fast?"

She nodded. "That would be nice."

Joe removed his hat and placed it on the empty chair next to him. "In order to get here, you had to travel twelve years."

"What?" Tangi counted on her fingers. "When I left Mimbeye I was thirteen years old. You mean now I'm twenty-five?"

"That's right. One day in the other world can be years in Rosevine. Now, let me tell you a story you've probably waited your whole life to hear. About your mother."

Tangi pushed the tea away and strained her ears. As she sat there, her eyes fixed on Joe's lined, animated face, she got to know her mother.

Chapter Thirteen
Welcome Home

"A princess? My mother?" Tangi couldn't help grinning.

"That's what she was, the only child born to the king and queen of Rosevine. As a child, they doted on her and did everything to protect her." He wiped his brow with a handkerchief as if telling the story was hard for him. "But when she turned thirteen, she wanted more. She yearned for her freedom and decided to go searching for it."

Tangi shifted her chair closer to the table, as if the words that came out of Joe's mouth couldn't reach her ears fast enough. "What happened then? Where did she go?"

"The search led her to the main gate of Rosevine. No one was ever allowed to walk out of it, but she did. She was a curious girl, your mother." Joe chuckled and the wrinkles around his eyes deepened. Then his face turned serious again. "She wandered too far into the desert and could no longer find the rose gate, so she sat by a small brook she came across and started to cry. Her tears fell into the water.

"After some time, she got too hot and stepped into the brook to cool down. Just like the way you travelled here, the same happened to her. She was swept into another world: Mimbeye."

"Daryle said she was never accepted there." As Joe had said, they had both been transported to another world through their tears, but unlike her, her mother had landed in a world where no one except her father cared for her. "Why didn't she just come back the same way she'd left?"

"Because she met your father, fell in love and refused to come back to Rosevine." Joe took a sip of his tea. "Rosevine was never the same without her. Many tears were shed. The queen fell ill not long after, and it wasn't long before she died, followed closely by the king, who died from a broken heart." Joe lifted his gaze to look at Tangi. "Your grandparents were the first people to die in Rosevine. It changed everything."

Tangi swallowed. Her mum had left behind so much pain just to be with her father? She must have loved him. Tangi was glad she did. If her mum had decided to come back to Rosevine, she would never have been born. "What changed?"

Joe didn't say anything for a while, just stared out the window. Then he cleared his throat. "Rosevine paid the price. Water was scarce and the sun dimmed, wilting the roses. People started to panic when the roses died.

Then something terrifying occurred. The people began to shrink. As long as Rosevine wasn't saved, they would keep shrinking until..." His voice trailed off into nothingness.

"Until?"

Joe's face clouded. "They would shrink until one day they just disappear."

Tangi flinched when she saw the touch of fear in Joe's eyes. He had already shrunk so much. How long until it was all over for him? Of course she couldn't ask him that.

Joe wiped his bald head. He looked sad now. "I used to be one of the strongest men in Rosevine, you know. Now, if Rosevine is not saved, I'll disappear, just like everyone else. Everyone shrinks at a different rate; some slower than others. The royal family shrinks the slowest."

Tangi stood, went over to Joe, and touched his arm. "I'm so sorry, Joe. I'm sure if my mother had known what was happening, she would have returned."

Joe shook his head. "She couldn't. As soon as she married a man who was not a Rosevien, the doors shut her out. She could never return, even if she'd wanted to."

"But I don't understand. My mum had left years ago. Why hasn't Rosevine disappeared yet?"

Joe's face softened and his eyes danced. "Something unexpected happened. A boy was born to a couple in Rosevine. The first baby in two decades. We named him Daryle, and his parents became the new king and queen of Rosevine because they brought us hope. You'll meet them tonight. They're great people."

"What happened next?"

"Time stopped for five years. No one shrunk, no rose died, and the sun got brighter."

"And Rosevine became beautiful again."

"Not quite. Its beauty can only be restored completely if the prince marries a child born by your mother. Since she had no other children, that leaves you. Tangi, we've been waiting for you for many years. Only you and Daryle can save Rosevine."

"I can't believe it. I'm a princess. A real princess." And something else had happened to her when she set foot in Rosevine. She hadn't on-ly grown physically; her voice was deeper than it used to be. She looked like a grownup and felt and thought like one.

"Yes, you are. And if you marry Daryle, you could become queen one day."

She crossed back to her seat, fell into it, her head buried in her hands. How could she marry Daryle? She didn't even know him. She wanted to save Rosevine, and she liked Daryle, but she didn't love him. The princesses in the stories she'd read had always been in love with their prince.

Tangi lifted her eyes to look back at Joe. "What if I don't marry him?"

"You'll still be the princess of Rosevine, but it will not be saved."

"What about my tears, can't they help?"

"Not if you don't marry the prince."

"Oh." Tangi's shoulders sagged. "Why are my tears important?"

"When your mother left, our people shed a lot of tears for her. Rosevine can only be saved if the tears of your mother's child replaced them. Three of our people had died; your mother and her parents. That's why you had to fill three bottles. One for each of them."

Tangi took a sip of her tea, which was now cold, and put the mug back down. "I want to help, Joe, but—"

Joe stood up from his chair and put his hat back on. "I know this is all too much information at once. You don't have to decide now. Take your time. Right now, you have a ball to dress for."

"A ball? But I don't have anything to wear."

"Yes you do, princess. Go along the corridor. The second room on the left is yours. There you'll find everything you need. Go on." Joe waved a hand and chuckled.

Tangi hesitated and then left the kitchen.

The room Joe directed her to was small and pretty, with a wooden cupboard in one corner. Next to it was a dresser with the largest mirror Tangi had ever seen. She moved closer and looked at herself properly, studying her new adult look. Then a glint in the mirror caught her attention. She spun on her heel. A beautiful yellow and white silk gown with diamond sparkles all over it lay on the bed. Beside it was an open box filled with glittering pieces of jewelry. She ran to the bed and lifted the dress to her face. The material was so soft, it felt like air on her cheek, and the diamonds so fine, like specks of dust.

She closed her eyes and whispered into the dress, "I can't believe I'm a princess."

"You better believe it," a familiar female voice came from the door.

She dropped the dress on the bed and spun around. Her heart almost jumped from her chest, then her eyes filled with tears. It couldn't be. "Fye?"

The small woman standing in front of Tangi resembled Fye, but older. "It's me, darling Tangi."

"What are you doing here? How did you find me?" Tangi bent down and hugged her friend, who was as short as Joe.

"This is my home. I'm Joe's wife."

Tangi let go of her. "You're what? You're from Rosevine?"

"Yes." Fye nodded and wiped her eyes. "And I'm so happy to see you. Now come on, we don't have much time. Let me help you get ready for the ball." Fye was already dressed in a flowing blue gown.

Fye had Tangi sit on the bed and climbed up

onto a small stool she pulled from underneath the bed, so she was at the same level as Tangi's head. She unraveled the plaits, freeing her hair one curl at a time.

"Why didn't you tell me about Rosevine in Mimbeye?"

"I didn't have the right to. I snuck out of Rosevine only because I wanted to see you, to watch out for you. If I did more than that, I would have been locked out forever."

"Why did you take such a great risk?"

"I loved your mother. When news of her death reached us, I knew I had to come to you. You are all that's left of her."

"I thought when you go to another world you travel for twelve years. Why did you turn into a child?"

"It works in opposites; I am an adult here, so became a child there. Your mother was a child here, so became an adult there."

Joe and Fye had given Tangi many answers yet she still had so many questions. There would be enough time later to get all the answers she wanted. "The most important thing is that we're together again."

Fye placed a small diamond and pearl tiara on top of Tangi's head. "Exactly. Princess, you can look now."

Tangi looked herself in the mirror and her mouth dropped open. She looked very pretty. The tiara topped off her bob of tight curls, which shone like spun silk. After she put on her gown and jewelry, she felt like a true princess. To complete the look, she slipped her feet into silver strappy sandals, holding Fye's hand for balance.

*

Before they left, Fye placed her hands on both sides of Tangi's face and looked at her. "Thanks for coming here. I didn't know if I'd ever see you again."

"Thank you too, for taking care of me in the other world."

Fye dabbed at a tear on her cheek. "No need to be emotional now. We've got a ball to go to." She took Tangi's hand and led her out of the room.

A small magnolia white boat, with Tangi's name printed on its side in gold lettering, waited for them on the riverbank. When they approached, a shiny silver staircase appeared, and they climbed up it and into the boat.

Tangi shook her head in amazement as she studied the shiny wooden flooring, the matching benches with gold engraved cushion padding, the pristine glass walls and roof.

Fye came to stand next to her. "Your grandfather had this built for you when he found out about your birth."

Tangi bit back tears. "And I thought no one except my father and uncle cared for me."

Joe lowered himself onto a bench in the corner and stretched his short legs out in front of him. "You have no idea. Every single one of the five thousand citizens of Rosevine loves you. Just you wait and see."

Once they had all settled in, the boat started gliding down the river, between the rows of hill houses.

By the time they reached the hall of celebrations, the sun had set. A band of pink, orange and red melted at the horizon, and the moon peered down at them from overhead.

Tangi heard the music first, mingled with the sound of water lapping at the sides of the boat. Then the hall came into focus as the boat floated closer. It was large, glass, and covered by crisscrossing white rose vines and ivy and sparkling fairy lights.

When the boat came to a halt, Joe climbed down the steps and led the way to the entrance, where another small man opened the doors for them.

Inside was even more beautiful than outside—marble floors, a cascading fountain, and rose petals that glowed as they floated in the air close to the ceiling.

They entered and the music stopped as everyone wheeled around to stare at Tangi. So ma-ny shades of brown skin—from the color of cof-fee beans to that of the caramels she used to buy from the village shop. Tall people, short people, and some who had shrunk so much they looked like children.

Tangi placed one foot carefully in front of the other. Her gaze darted from face to face but she didn't look into the eyes of the people who expected her to save them. She couldn't bear seeing the slivers of fresh hope mirrored in them. The hope that she would save Rosevine, save them. What if she couldn't? Her mouth went dry.

Fye squeezed Tangi's hand and it gave her the confidence she needed. She was not alone. Rosevine was her home. She swallowed hard through the tightness in her throat and lifted her gaze. She had nothing to fear. No pressure. *Just keep walking.* Gathering her gown in her hands, not because it was too long but because she wanted something to hold for reassurance, she continued.

Then she reached a raised platform at the front of the hall, with carpeted steps leading up to it.

"Welcome home, Tangi. I'm King Smineon." He leaned forward in his engraved golden throne and met her eyes. He had sprinkles of gray in his hair and his eyes reminded her of Uncle Thomas', warm and comforting, like the honey Mrs. Namula had sometimes smeared on the bread she had given Tangi to take to school. When he smiled, the skin around his eyes crinkled. "Come on up."

The fear melted and she smiled back. She ascended the steps, the small heels of her sandals hushing as they sank into the carpet, and came to stand in front of him.

How did one greet a king? She kicked herself for not asking Fye. She stretched out her hand toward him. "It's nice to meet you, King Smineon."

Instead of shaking her hand, King Smineon straightened the crown on his head, then rose fluidly from his throne. He walked forward and kissed her on the forehead. His voice cracked when he spoke. "I'm the one who's happy to meet you. But I'm not the only one." He guided her toward a beautiful woman that sat in a throne next to his. "This is Lorea, my wife."

Tangi had never seen anyone more beautiful. Long dark eyelashes framed her almond-shaped velvet brown eyes, and her skin, flawless as the surface of a rose petal, made her fingertips tingle with the urge to touch it. The silk fabric of her powder blue embroidered gown gathered in folds at her feet, like water cascading into a plunge pool.

She too stood up and kissed Tangi on the forehead. Then she hugged her, and Tangi thought she'd never let go. When she did, her eyes glistened with moisture. "Welcome home, Tangi." Queen Lorea lowered herself back down onto the throne.

"There's someone else you should meet."

King Smineon now led her to the other end of the platform, where a handsome man sat. More handsome than when she had seen him in the pond. Short, curly, coal black hair, the same color as his eyes, and a clean-shaven face. One hand rested casually on the armrest of his silver throne. When she approached, he rose to his feet and kissed both her cheeks. "We finally meet in person."

Her hands twisted unconsciously together as she looked up at him. They wanted her to marry him but she didn't feel anything more than friendship.

"Come and sit next to me." Daryle broke through her thoughts. He took her elbow and led her to the other silver throne, the one next to his.

"This is where you belong."

Tangi's knees buckled and she almost collapsed onto the padded seat. How did this all happen to her, the girl that limped, the one everybody saw right through? How was it possible that she was now an adult, with perfect legs, surrounded by people that had been dying to meet her and a prince that wanted to marry her? For a moment she feared it was all a dream, a creation of her imagination, and any minute now she would wake up. But it wasn't.

"Ladies and gentlemen!" King Smineon faced the eager faces below the platform. "It's time to raise a toast to Princess Tangi, and give her a proper welcome home."

Princess. Despite the crown in her hair, Tangi had not yet truly come to terms with this. But then, that was exactly what she was. Her mother was a princess and that made her one too.

Daryle reached out and squeezed her hand. Then crystal glasses with a peach-colored liquid appeared in everyone's hands.

When everyone had theirs, they lifted them in her direction. "To you, Princess."

Tangi gave a small nod and waved down at them. She then lifted the glass to her lips and hesitated.

Daryle tinkled his glass against hers. "It's rose wine but there's no trace of alcohol inside."

How had he known that was what she had been wondering? Tangi nodded and tasted her drink. Mildly sweet, fizzy, delicious.

Daryle drained his glass. "Are you ready to greet everyone else?"

Tangi swallowed and raised an eyebrow. "All those people?" Tangi gazed down at the expectant faces on both sides of the aisle.

"I'm sure they're all anxious to meet you close up." He gave a little chuckle. "I'll go down with you if that would make you less nervous."

Tangi drained her glass as well. Then she looked for a place to put the empty glass, but it vanished from her hand, leaving only air in its place. Uncurling her fingers, she surveyed her empty palm in amazement.

She looked up at Daryle's amused eyes. "What happened?"

"Don't worry. You'll get used to things like that happening. Shall we go down?" Daryle got to his feet and extended his hand to her.

Tangi gave her hand another brief look, then nodded. "Okay."

She let him lead her down the steps and they disappeared into the throng of people.

As Tangi shook one hand after the other—some big, some small—she couldn't believe she had been nervous. The Rosevien people embraced her with so much love. Some even hugged her or kissed her hand, making her feel even more that she belonged. For the first time in her life, she belonged.

"Nice to meet you, Princess. My name is Pauline. Your mother was a sweet girl, very intelligent." A small, old, twinkle-eyed woman grasped her hand. "I was her teacher, taught her everything she knew."

Talking to these people was the best thing. They made her feel closer to her mother.

"I was their cook right until the end." Tangi's chest ached as she looked into the deep set, lusterless eyes of a wrinkled man who had introduced himself as Moran. The death of the royal family had clearly scarred him.

"What do you do now?" She just couldn't help asking.

"I'm too old and too shrunken to do anything. All I do is grow my vegetables and wait for the end. But you're here now…to save us."

Lovely as it was to talk to everyone, every conversation ended the same and left Tangi feeling as if a pile of bricks dropped onto her back, weighing her down. How would she ever live with herself if she didn't help them?

Half an hour later, King Smineon announced that dinner was ready. As soon as the words left his mouth, high-backed white velvet chairs replaced the ordinary metal ones. A long buffet table appeared on one side of the hall, covered with flowing silk covers in royal blue. A variety of food covered the table tops— breads, meats, cakes, fruits, vegetables and sweets and so much more. Tangi had never seen such a feast. The round dinner tables were also draped with royal blue tablecloths and topped with candles standing on silver mirrors, sprinkled with rhinestones and blue rose petals. She had also never heard of blue roses, but then again, she had never seen or heard about most of the things she saw in Rosevine.

Stop questioning everything and just enjoy yourself, she mentally cajoled.

As she took her seat, the lights dimmed and the hall transformed into a blue, white and silver fairytale. Even the fountain had a blue glow to it.

She placed her elbow on the table, rested her chin in her hand and took it all in. "This is all so beautiful."

"Yes, it is. And it's all for you. We haven't

had a celebration like this in years."

Tangi knew why. There had been nothing to celebrate. "Thank you."

"No." Daryle's voice was a hushed whisper. "Thank *you*. Now I'm sure you're hungry."

Tangi's stomach growled in answer and her cheeks heated up.

Daryle touched her hand. "Don't worry, no one else heard. Forget about it."

Soon everyone had taken their seats, and the room was noisy with clinking silverware, murmuring, and even soft birdsong. This time, the food only appeared in front of the royal family. The rest of the guests had to fetch their own food from the buffet. They didn't seem to mind as they whispered and laughed as they scooped and piled their plates with all kinds of food.

As they ate, Daryle and Queen Lorea told Tangi a little more about her mother, Daryle from what he'd heard and his mother from knowing her personally.

The way that they spoke of her, by the time Tangi had finished the meal, she felt as if she had known her mother all her life. She couldn't have asked for a better gift from anyone. And at the same time, she felt as though she had known everyone here for a lifetime, too.

*

The celebration went beyond dinner. When the food had disappeared, most of the tables and chairs vanished too and the party started. First, a few people sang or danced for Tangi as a gift. Then her eyes filled with tears as she watched a group of wrens singing her a song. She had always known birds to sing beautiful tunes, but this was something else.

The female birds began the song, then the males joined in. The birds sang together back and forth, taking turns as the tune went along. Finally they chirped at such a fast rate that the tunes melted into each other and it seemed as if only one bird was singing. The most beautiful thing was that with each verse, the birds bobbed their heads and flew closer together. The crowd cheered every time they did, and so did Tangi, who stood in the middle of the hall between Fye and Joe.

At midnight, the singing stopped and the room burst with the sound of clapping and cheering.

The birds bobbed their heads a final time and, in single file, flew out the door.

"You look like you're having fun."

Tangi looked up to see Daryle gazing down at her. "I've never had this much fun. Ever."

"I'm glad to hear that. Do you want to go for a walk, talk a bit?"

"Sure. That would be nice."

First they just strolled side by side in silence,

along the banks of a nearby lake, watching the golden glow of the moonlight melting onto the surface of the water like liquid gold. The soft night breeze stroked her face and shoulders.

"Should we take a seat?" Daryle gestured to a wooden bench.

Tangi sat down, but her eyes stayed glued to the lake that glowed in the dark. "It's so beautiful here, so peaceful."

"You're more beautiful," Daryle replied. "Tangi, I know Joe has told you everything. I wish you would marry me. Not just to save Rosevine, but because I love you. I've loved you from the first time I heard your name when I was just a little boy."

Tangi looked at him through the moonlight. "How can you love someone you haven't met?"

He took her hand into his. "You can if you were born to love that person."

"But don't I have to love you in return in order to marry you?"

"I wouldn't force you to do anything you don't want. Also, Rosevine cannot be saved if our marriage is not out of love."

If only she knew how much time it took for someone to fall in love. Daryle had loved her since he was a child. That was many years. What if she needed just as long?

"How much time do I have? How much time is left before Rosevine disappears?"

Daryle let go of her hand and stood up,

facing the lake. "A month. If we are not married by then, Rosevine will disappear at midnight, on this month's last day."

"That's too little time."

He nodded. "I know, and I wish I could give us more."

Tangi sighed. "How can I know for sure that we are meant for each other? How can I fall in love with you in just four weeks?"

His eyes sparkled. "I love you, but I'll never force you into anything. That's why I want to do this the right way."

Tangi raised an eyebrow. "What do you mean?"

"We have a few weeks to get to know each other. Maybe we can go on a few dates."

"I've never been on a date before." In fact, until arriving here she hadn't known what a date even was. This was one of the new things her mind had been equipped with.

"Me neither. So, what do you say, should we go on our first date?"

"I think that's a brilliant idea. I'd love to get to know you better." She paused. "But what will happen to me if I can't save Rosevine? Will I disappear too?"

"No, you will be given the choice of going back to Mimbeye."

Her eyes grew wide. "But you said I will get hurt as long as I'm there."

He was quiet for a moment before he stopped and faced her. "I'd rather you go back there and live than disappear forever."

*

Back inside the hall, the music had died down and the guests trickled out.

Tangi sat back at the royal table and Queen Lorea came to join her.

"I wanted to let you know that if you would like, you can move into the castle tonight. Your rooms are ready for you."

"My rooms?" Tangi had never had a room that was all her own. Now she was getting several? "I have more than one?"

The queen chuckled. "You are a princess."

Tangi didn't want to sound ungrateful but she couldn't accept the offer. "Do I have to move tonight?"

"No, you don't have to. I just thought you'd like to make yourself at home."

Tangi wasn't ready to do that. She had just met them today. "I'd like to stay with Fye and Joe for a while, if that's all right."

The queen patted her hand. "When you're ready, you're welcome anytime."

"Thank you."

Fifteen minutes later, Tangi bade farewell and left in her boat with Joe and Fye.

Before she fell asleep, she ran the events of the day in her head. Her transformation into a new person with an older mind. A *new* mind: she had come across things she had never encountered, yet knew what they were. Almost as if the information had been planted into her head.

It all felt like a dream and she was just waiting to wake up.

Chapter Fourteen
Tinsel In The Sky

Golden light flooded the room, but Tangi wasn't ready to get up. She needed to enjoy the warmth and softness of the bed just a little longer. The bed was large and the cotton sheets felt like soft feathers against her skin.

As she snuggled under the covers, a soft tap at the window caught her attention.

It was a white dove, perched on a branch. Its small round eyes stared at her. In its beak it held a tiny piece of rolled up paper.

She swept the sheets to one side and jumped out of bed. She opened the window and placed her hand under the dove's beak. It dropped the paper in the palm of her hand. She wrapped her fingers around it and stroked the dove's head with the finger of her other hand. It moved its small head against her finger, enjoying her touch. Then it gently pecked at the hand Tangi held the paper in.

"You want me to open it, don't you?"

The dove bobbed its head.

"All right then." She unrolled the paper and read.

Princess Tangi, let's go on our first date. I'd love to show you Rosevine. I'll see you at noon.

Tangi returned her attention to the dove. "Thank you, little… bird, for bringing me the message."

The dove made a nodding movement, stepped back, and then flew away.

She followed its flight over the lush grass and flower-covered rooftops. All of them had a small round chimney sticking out. Plumes of smoke curled out of some of them and floated up into the wide open sky.

Just as she turned her back to the window, Fye walked in with a tray laden with food. "Good morning, Princess." She placed the tray on the stool at the end of the bed. "How was your first night in Rosevine?"

Tangi went over to Fye and hugged her. "It was the best night of my life."

"I'm so happy to hear that." Fye stepped back and touched Tangi's hand. "Mine too."

Tangi raised an eyebrow. "Why is that?"

"I never thought I'd see my best friend's daughter in Rosevine, let alone in my own home. It's like having your mother here. It means a lot to me."

"It means more to me. Talking to you and the other people last night made me feel so much closer her."

Fye fluffed the pillows and straightened the bed sheets. "They all love you so much. Just as much as they loved your mother. By the way, any plans for the day? If not, I can show you around."

"I got a note, actually. From Daryle. He's offered to show me Rosevine. I'm meeting him at noon."

"You mean he wants to be near you."

"Whatever his motives are, it's nice of him. I look forward to seeing everything."

"Great. Let's get you ready, then."

Tangi tipped her head to one side and narrowed her eyes.

"Why are you looking at me like that?" Fye asked.

"Why are you doing all this?" Tangi skimmed the bed and looked at Fye.

"What?"

Tangi perched on the edge of the bed. "You're acting like my maid. You cook for me, make my bed, help me dress...I just wonder if...."

Fye climbed onto the bed and sat next to her. "I do it because I love taking care of you. I'll continue to do so as long as you want me to."

"That's so kind of you, Fye." Tangi shifted on the bed. "Did you do the same for my mother?"

"I used to babysit your mother. I was just a teenager at the time." Fye's face was bleak with sorrow. "I loved taking care of her, just like I love taking care of you now. Please let me."

"Thank you. I'll let you do things for me, on one condition." Tangi put an arm around Fye's small shoulders. "You're not my babysitter or my maid, but my friend. Is that all right with you?"

"That's fine." Fye climbed with a little difficulty off the high bed and patted Tangi's knee. "Your prince will be picking you up in less than an hour. I'm afraid you'll have to eat your breakfast while I help you get ready."

Fye walked over to the wardrobe, climbed up onto a stool and pulled out a knee length aquamarine dress. The bust was covered with milky pearls.

Tangi felt so special. It all felt like a dream. She could easily get used to living this way, eating great food and wearing beautiful clothes.

She wished so much she could fall in love with Daryle. He was handsome and kind, and a prince. Four weeks. If she could get to know him, grow to love him, in that time, Rosevine would be saved.

*

When Tangi stepped out of the house at noon, she almost tripped as she came face to face with a giant bird. It was another dove, but this time enormous, its eyes as big as saucers.

Daryle was sitting on top of it, smiling down at her. He had a dimple. She hadn't noticed it before.

As she stood there, thunderstruck, the dove

bent its knees and lowered itself to the ground. He hopped off and kissed her cheek. "It's nice to see you."

"You too." She wasn't looking at him but at the bird. What if she slid off and fell to her death?

"Ready to go?" He stretched out his hand to help her up.

Tangi nodded and chewed on her bottom lip. This was the most frightening thing she'd ever had to do in her life. How would she ever be ready?

Daryle narrowed his eyes a fraction. "You're not afraid of heights, are you?"

"I don't know...I've never flown before."

"Maybe it's time you gave it a go, then. Flying is one of the most common modes of transport here. You don't have to be afraid."

Tangi looked from him to the bird. Then she drew a breath and grasped his hand. "Let's go."

In one swift motion, he swept her off the ground and pulled her onto the dove's back. There was a white cushioned seat, which she nestled into, nervously eyeing it to ensure it was properly secured.

"Don't worry." Daryle hopped onto the dove's back. "It's perfectly safe."

"But how's that possible? The seat isn't attached."

"Since you came to Rosevine, a few things have happened we never thought possible. Let this be one of them. Trust me, Tinsel will keep us safe."

"Tinsel?"

"The dove."

"Nice name." Unusual, too. But this was Rosevine. The rules of normality didn't seem to apply.

As Tinsel straightened, Tangi gritted her teeth. When the dove started running and then lifted off the ground, his wings spread out like two giant fans, she reached out and clutched Daryle's hand.

Tinsel sliced through the air with ease and glided over the river, between the hill houses, following it as if it were a road to somewhere. Rising higher, the air became cooler, more refreshing. Though Tinsel moved at great speed, the air around them seemed still, barely caressing them with a light breeze. At the same time, Tangi did not feel herself moving even an inch from the unsecured seat. But she still refused to look below the level of her eyes. She fixed them on the scene in the distance of the round-tipped grassy hills meeting the baby blue sky.

They passed two other enormous birds on their flight. One was black and white, and the other had dull brown feathers which wore thin in some places. Even for someone who didn't live in Rosevine, it was easy to see that Tinsel, with his full, well-groomed cotton-white feathers, and impressive size—he was as big as the two others put together—was no ordinary bird. He belonged to the royal family.

Each bird had one passenger on board, one a small man with beard reaching up to his chest and the other a woman with an afro puff. Both birds slowed down when Tinsel approached them and the passengers bowed their heads before speeding off again.

After ten minutes, Daryle said, "Will you be okay or should we go back down?"

Tangi shook her head. "No. I'm fine…I'll be fine." How could she say no to him? He was making an effort to show her around, make her feel at home.

"You don't look it. Actually, I know what would help. Hang on a second." He extracted his hand from her grip and pulled out an olive green bottle and two long slender crystal glasses from somewhere at his feet.

Tangi was pretty sure there had been nothing at their feet when she'd taken her seat.

He unscrewed the cap and poured the lime colored liquid in both glasses, then gave her one of them. "Whenever I was scared or nervous as a child, my mum made me drink one of these. It always worked wonders." He gave a small wink. "See for yourself."

"What's it made of?" Tangi frowned but lifted the glass until it touched her lips. For a greenish drink, it had a light chocolaty smell.

He raised an eyebrow. "Have a guess."

Tangi tipped the glass against her lips and the drink flowed into her mouth. Eyes narrowed, she ran it over her tongue for a bit. "Chocolate? Some type of fruit. And is that ... ginger?"

"Chocolate, for sure. There are also, and you won't believe this, twenty different types of roses in that drink."

"Roses? You mean real ones?"

"Yes. Just like the rose wine we had last night; that was made of almost seventy kinds of roses."

"Wow. I had no idea roses are edible."

Daryle drank from his glass, then wiped his lips with the back of his hand. "There are around ten thousand rose species in Rosevine. About half of them can be eaten."

"That's amazing." Tangi drank some more. "Are the edible ones only used to make drinks?"

"No, they can also be used for cooking and baking all kinds of things like soups, stews, cakes, anything really. But they are only used in the preparation of food that will be shared by all the Roseviens at celebrations hosted by the king and queen. If consumed at private occasions, they can cause someone to fall very ill and to shrink a couple of inches more."

Tangi eyed her glass. "Why are we consuming them privately then?"

"There are exceptions." He drained his glass. "The royal family is allowed to consume a certain amount of the roses per year."

"I see. Looks like the royal family gets a lot of special treatment around here. You shrink slowest and you get to eat roses."

Daryle threw back his head and let out a great peal of laughter. "Well, it does have its advantages." Then he stopped laughing and his face became all serious. "But when our people suffer, we suffer too."

Tangi stiffened. She and her big mouth. She'd just told him the royal family was spoiled. "Of course. Sorry, I didn't mean it like that."

Daryle's face loosened. "Of course you didn't. You shouldn't feel bad. So, how do you feel now?"

Feel? Incredibly, she had totally forgotten about her fear. Without her even noticing it, the nervous butterflies that invaded her stomach just a few minutes ago had disappeared and the fear had crumbled like the hut she had seen in the desert. She gave Daryle a large grin. "I actually feel good." She drained her glass. "It really does work."

"Or maybe it's talking to me that did the trick."

It was her turn to laugh. How could it be that she'd met Daryle in person just yesterday? Inside her heart, it was as if she'd known him for a lifetime. She felt so comfortable with him—but just comfortable.

"Do you want more?"

"No, I'm fine." Tangi handed him her empty glass. Daryle simply threw it overboard, along with his own. Tangi followed them with her eyes until, suddenly, they vanished.

"Where did they go?"

"Back to the castle."

"Can I send the bottle to the castle too?"

"Sure." Daryle handed it to her.

Tossing it overboard, Tangi watched until it, too, disappeared. "Wow," she breathed. She was in awe, but not because of the bottle disappearing, even if that was amazing, but because of the scene that met her eyes as she looked down lower.

Below them, endless rivers shone and a sea of multicolored roses mingled with various shades of green. The air above Rosevine glinted in the bright sunlight, making all the colors even brighter. She regretted not having looked down sooner. She looked back up at Daryle. "It's so beautiful. By the way, where are you taking me?"

"To the other side of Rosevine. A place I don't like to visit unless I have to."

"If you don't like going to that place, why are you taking me there?"

"It will help you understand what's going on. We won't spend too much time there."

Ten minutes later, Tangi knew what Daryle meant. The green hills and colorful roses had vanished. A whole new scene stretched out below them, a scene of browns and greys. The trees had no leaves. The grass was dead.

Tinsel angled his flight, speeding downward now. The bare treetops got closer, then Tangi spotted a clearing below as Tinsel sank down through the parted branches. Slowing to a halt, Tinsel landed lightly in the clearing in the woods. Daryle leapt off and offered her his hand. It was big and strong and warm to the touch.

Once on the ground, she was able to take a closer look at her surroundings.

No wonder Daryle had said this was the other side of Rosevine. It was dull and lifeless, like the desert she had seen yesterday. The air smelled different too—like rotting wood, dead flowers, and stagnant water.

She took a small step away from the dry grass that tickled her ankle. "What is this place?"

Daryle took hold of her arm as they walked. "This is the part that has died off. If we don't save the Kingdom, it will disintegrate and become just like this. The decay is spreading fast."

Dead twigs crunched under Tangi's feet as she walked. "I didn't think it was this bad."

How could such a beautiful place be transformed into something that resembled a graveyard? Everything was dead. Anything still standing was a dirty and rotten brown. Dry branches creaked, and she winced out of fear that they could just let go of their trunks at any second. The rivers had also run dry or become tainted with mud.

"This is terrible."

Daryle circumvented the interlaced threads of a spider's web. "Yes, it is."

Tangi stopped walking. She drew a deep breath and bunched her hands into fists to stop them from trembling. "Daryle, we will save Rosevine. I'm willing to do anything."

This was where her mother had been born. The closest she had ever come to knowing her. She had to make sure it was safe and cherished. In order for her mother's memories to be preserved, Rosevine had to exist beyond just a month.

His dark eyebrows slanted in a frown. "What are you saying?"

She took his hands. "I'll marry you if I have to." In the fairytale books she used to read, no girl ever refused to marry a handsome prince.

"No, Tangi." Daryle let go of her hands and put his on her shoulders. "That's not why I brought you here. I don't want you to do anything you're not sure about. I want to marry you for love, from both sides."

"Then why did you bring me here?"

"I just wanted to show you that Rosevine was not all that it seemed. Only by coming here can one appreciate the fragile beauty that's left."

They started walking again.

"You know something?" She watched him from the corner of her eye.

"No, what is it?"

"I kind of regret coming here, to Rosevine. If I didn't, Rosevine could still get a chance to exist for maybe a few more years. I've just made the clock tick faster."

"It's not your fault. It was going to happen at some point. For now let's just be positive."

As they walked on, Daryle told Tangi more stories about her mother when she was a child.

"My mother told me she was beautiful, bubbly, smart, and always one step ahead of the kids her age."

"That must be what led her out of the gate. While everyone was content, she probably wanted to see more of the world, to quench her curiosity."

"Maybe." His voice mixed with the creaking of the branches. "I'm sorry you never got a chance to really know her."

"Me too."

He stopped next to a moss-covered tree trunk that stank of death. "See that?" He pointed ahead of them.

Her gaze followed his finger to a crumbling castle. Half of it was covered in dead branches, and the other half looked as if it would crumble at any moment.

"That was your grandparents' castle. Your mother was born there."

She caught her breath, and her knees weakened. "That was my mother's home?" Her voice came out a little hoarse.

"Yes, until she left."

Tangi gazed at the castle. This crumbling mess had once been intact, strong. She imagined her mother as a little girl, running up and down the steps that led to the castle, until one day she descended them for the last time.

"Thank you for bringing me here. This means so much." And it did. Despite the rot, the decay and crumble, these were her roots. There was no place she would rather be.

"Why don't we get a closer look?"

They walked down a path strewn with dead leaves and twigs and climbed up the flight of cracked steps. There were maybe twenty or thirty of them. In Mimbeye, Tangi never would have been able to climb these steps, owing to her short leg.

She gulped for breath. "I can't believe my ... family used to climb these steps every day."

Daryle didn't look flustered at all. "They didn't need to. They flew."

"They flew?"

"No." He shook his head and laughed. "Not what you think. On birds, remember?"

"Oh yes, I forgot about that."

Even if most of the castle was destroyed, a large portion still had intact stone block walls.

They climbed another few steps. Then they

stood in front of double wooden doors.

With the flat of her hand, Tangi shoved the doors open. Dust flew out and coated her nose and mouth and she coughed. She also squinted so her eyelashes could catch the dust before it entered her eyes.

Stepping in further, broken glass crunched under her shoes.

Daryle moved closer to her. "You okay?"

She nodded, but her emotions swirled inside of her and she felt the signs of a headache coming on. Being here was upsetting. Her family's memories were now nothing but crumbling ruins. The only sign the place had ever been lived in was broken and decaying furniture.

Daryle and Tangi stepped over a large gap in the floorboards. She almost lost her balance, but he caught her.

He didn't let go of her elbow as they climbed up the creaky staircase, dodging cobwebs.

Tangi sighed. "Isn't it funny how a person can live one moment and be gone the next?"

"I'm sorry you had to lose your parents. It's not fair."

"At least I gained new friends."

Daryle wrapped an arm around her shoulder. "And a new family."

Tangi stopped walking and looked into his deep brown eyes. She felt a flutter inside her stomach. Could this be love? How could she know?

She peeled her gaze from Daryle's and opened a creaking door. A spacious room stretched out in front of them. But beyond dust and cobwebs, there was little to see.

She walked over the debris to the window and squinted through the dirty broken glass into the dead garden. In her mind's eye, she saw children playing hide and seek, hiding behind pruned hedges, as their parents looked on. One of those children was her mother.

Daryle came over to where she was standing and looked out. "From what I've been told, this garden was one of the most beautiful in the whole Kingdom. The doors were always kept open for Roseviens to have picnics and garden parties."

"I'm sure it was lovely."

"Okay." He rubbed his hands together. "Enough sadness. I have an idea that could cheer you up. Come with me."

Tangi followed him out of the room, down the stairs, and out the door into the garden.

He stopped and turned to her, a huge grin on his face. "We should have a picnic."

"A picnic?" She eyed the dead grass, weeds, and debris all around them. "Here?"

"I can't think of a better place. Watch this." Daryle lowered his gaze to the ground and made a sweeping hand motion.

A fleece blanket appeared on the ground at their feet. On top of it lay a picnic basket covered with a loaf of bread, fruits, sausages, cheeses, and a bottle of grape juice. All around the blanket, the grass was greener and adorned with scattered baby flowers.

"How do you keep doing that?" Tangi asked, impressed.

"It's simple. Let's sit down." Both of them lowered onto the blanket. "It's all in the mind. You decide what you want, believe you can have it, and it happens."

Daryle unpacked the basket, spreading the food out on the blanket. He poured Tangi a drink and handed it to her.

"This is fascinating. I wish I could do it."

"Don't worry, you'll learn. It's all about believing you can have whatever it is that you want."

Tangi picked up a strawberry and bit into it. "I hope you're right. There are many things I would love to make happen in the blink of an eye."

How ironic, she thought. The Roseviens could make anything happen, except saving their kingdom: the thing they needed most.

Daryle grinned and his dimple fluttered on his left cheek, making him look like a little boy. "It will happen. You'll just need a little time."

Once the picnic was eaten and the leftovers vanished away, he showed her the grounds of the castle. Then Tinsel appeared to fly them back to the other side.

As the bird sliced through the sky, Tangi observed Daryle from the corner of her eye. She'd enjoyed spending time with him, couldn't have wished for a better way to spend the day. He was a good man, and any woman who married him would be very lucky.

"Let's get married," she blurted out, surprising not only him, but also herself.

"I don't understand." His brows drew together in confusion. "I didn't expect you to fall in love with me just after one date. I—"

"I'm not. I mean I like you ... very much. I just thought we have to do it, Daryle. We have to save Rosevine."

"Yes, but we have to be in love or it won't work."

"I know. We have thirty days."

"That's right." Daryle still looked confused.

"Well, we might as well get engaged now. I'll be in love with you by then." After all, he'd said if she believed hard enough for something to happen, it would. She wanted to fall in love with him. She wanted to save Rosevine. And it was going to happen.

"How do you know that?"

"I just do," she said.

For the rest of the ride to Joe and Fye's house, he didn't say a word. It left her feeling a little embarrassed. Had she said something wrong?

When they landed, Daryle helped her off

Tinsel and walked her to the door.

She faced him, wringing her hands. "I'm sorry if I said something wrong earlier."

He smiled and looked into her eyes. "No, you didn't. I just wanted to do this right. I was quiet because I was practicing my lines." He dropped to his knees. "Make me the happiest prince, Tangi. Will you marry me?"

He proposed to her just the way she'd seen princes doing in fairytales.

"Yes." The words flowed out of her mouth before she could stop them.

Daryle shut his eyes for a moment. When he reopened them, a brilliant diamond ring appeared on her finger.

Her heart warmed up inside her chest. Whether that was love, she didn't know.

Daryle stood up, a large grin on his face. "If everything goes well and our Kingdom is returned to its former glory, you and I will move into your grandparents' castle. I'll make sure it's completely repaired."

"Really? That would mean so much to me." She couldn't have asked for a better wedding gift.

"I thought it would."

*

That evening, King Smineon announced the engagement. His deep voice carried on the wings of the air over Rosevine and the Kingdom exploded with music, dancing and celebration.

When Tangi went to bed that night, she tried to believe that she would fall in love with Daryle before the thirty days were up, that she would not disappoint the Roseviens.

The next morning Fye and Tangi practiced wishing her dream wedding gown into reality. She'd seen a couple of wedding dresses in shop windows on the few visits to town with her father, and she had peered into the window of a bridal shop on her visit to Lorimi with Uncle Thomas.

"It's simple when you know what you want. Try again. You're a Rosevien; you can do it just like everybody else. Once you see it in your mind, it will appear in reality."

"You all had practice from birth. I didn't."

Fye shrugged. "That's not important. What matters is that you're a Rosevien. You have it in you."

Tangi sighed and closed her eyes again. This was her fourth time trying. She squeezed her eyes and forced images of her wedding gown into her mind.

"It's not working. All I can see are shadows."

Sometimes she did see images, but not ones strong enough to be able to translate into reality. It was not enough to just see her gown in her mind. She had to believe without a doubt that it would appear.

Fye had offered to create the wedding gown,

wanted Tangi to tell her what she wanted and she would make it a reality.

Tangi refused. Creating something out of nothing was as easy as breathing in Rosevine. If she was to fit in completely, she would have to learn to do it too.

She would also be creating her own bridal bouquet. She wanted to feel the fragility and softness of each petal. And to make the single flowers stronger than they'd been separately. Just as she was stronger now, together with people who loved and accepted her.

Chapter Fifteen
Blossoms

On their second date, Daryle took Tangi on a boat ride down the river.

It was a refreshing day, the air crisp and smelling of sweet grass and flowers. The clear water lapped the side of the boat as it bobbed along the river.

Daryle sat on the opposite side, whistling as he rowed. He'd been rowing for at least fifteen minutes without a single sign he was tired.

Tangi pretended to be interested in the deer that drank at the water's edge, the swirling water, the people stopping to work in their gardens to gaze after them, the grass waving in the breeze, the red and gold butterflies. All that did interest her, but what interested her most of all was Daryle—his chiseled face, brown eyes, long dark eyelashes, his strong shoulders. Her future husband. He was so handsome.

Closing her eyes, she enjoyed the warmth of the sun on her face and the sound of the leaves rustling in the trees. "I think this is a great idea. If we're to get married, I need to know more about you. You have the upper hand since you already seem to know everything about me."

Daryle stopped whistling. "I'm not as exciting as you think."

"Maybe you are; you just don't see it."

"All right, what do you want to know?"

Tangi opened her eyes. "Favorite drink?"

"Water." If he was joking, he didn't show it.

"You're joking, right? Of all the many delicious drinks that are available here?"

He stopped rowing but his hands remained on the oars. "Every other drink has a portion of water mixed in it. Someone has got to give it some credit, don't you think?"

She dipped a hand into the water. "You do have a point. Next question, what's your favorite color?"

"I can't really say. My favorites change often."

"Fair enough. Now, what's it like being a prince? Is it tough?"

"Apart from the fact that I live in a castle, I lead a pretty normal life. I don't have to do anything I don't want."

"But aren't you being forced to marry me?" Maybe he wasn't really in love with her, just doing what he had to. After all, it was a matter of life and death.

Daryle captured her gaze with his and for a moment he studied her intently. "The first time I saw your face, I felt drawn to you, even as a child. After that, I couldn't get enough of seeing you."

"How did you get to see me?"

"In dreams. It was hard to see you suffer and not being able to do anything. When Fye told me that she was thinking of going to be with you, I helped her escape."

"Thanks, Daryle. That was really nice of you to do."

"You're welcome. But then again, I didn't only do it for you. I did it for myself as well. When you hurt, I hurt. I've been waiting for you for a long time."

"I see." She watched him. How would it feel to love him the same way he loved her? Was it at all possible? He had loved her for years; to her, loving a man was still alien. But the clock was ticking. She had to do it.

He started to row again. "Before I forget, you're invited to dinner tonight at the castle."

"Sure, I'd like that. What time?"

"How about we go straight there with the boat? I could show you around the castle, since you haven't seen it yet."

"That sounds good."

*

The castle was built on concrete piers and nestled high on a hill, overlooking the river and surrounded by a beautiful garden and green fields. Every room Daryle showed Tangi made her feel welcome, at home.

To fill the time before dinner, they sat talking in the garden. He told her about his life as a prince and his passion for painting. She enjoyed being around him. Even when they didn't talk, just enjoyed the view of manicured lawns seeded with flowers, she felt calm, safe and comfortable around him.

She plucked a forget-me-not from its stem at her feet and stroked the petals with her forefinger. "I could sit here forever."

"And create flower arrangements?"

Tangi shook her head. "Is there anything you don't know about me?"

He chuckled. "Not really."

"Yes, you have very beautiful flowers here. They would make great bouquets and wreaths."

Daryle stood up. "In that case, there's something you should see."

He took her up onto the open rooftop. Tangi clapped a hand to her mouth as she stared at a beautiful garden filled with every flower imaginable — daisies, hydrangeas, pansies and countless types of roses. She stared in awe at the magnificence of the colors.

"Wow. This is amazing."

"I know. I had this garden made for you years ago, when I found out you appreciated flowers."

"You did this?"

"I wanted you to be happy when you got here. These flowers can't be found anywhere else in Rosevine. The best gardener in Rosevine comes here several times a week to take care of them."

What Daryle had done touched the deepest part of her. Not knowing how else to thank him, she threw herself into his arms and hugged him for a long time. "Thank you so much."

*

The days melted into each other and Tangi had never been happier. Sometimes she even forgot that Rosevine was like a glass on the edge of a table, on the verge of falling off.

Two weeks after arriving in Rosevine, she moved into the castle, and it soon became her home. Everyone made her feel like she was a missing part in their lives.

Soon, when she thought of Mimbeye, only the good memories settled on her mind—moments spent with Papa and Uncle Thomas, Fye, and Mrs. Namula's twins.

As everybody settled into their lives, she created her own routine. Most weekdays, she spent hours in the rooftop garden. She created flower arrangements to decorate the castle or just sat and admired the blossoms. The garden soon became a haven she retreated to, her secret garden.

Daryle spent most of his days helping rebuild the castle they would be moving into once married. He made sure Tangi was involved in every way. They spent endless hours, discussing how they would decorate their home and the types of flowers that Tangi would like to have in the garden. The garden he had made for her at the king and queen's castle, they decided, would be transferred to their new castle by wishing.

"Instead of rebuilding the castle by hand, why don't you just make a wish?"

"It won't be the same. Just because we have the choice of having anything we want without having to lift a finger, we don't have to take the shortcut. As you've seen, we enjoy doing most of the things by ourselves. Food cooked or a house built by hand is more precious."

"It does make sense. I think you're right."

Daryle's explanations always made her see things more clearly. She enjoyed their conversations so much and each passing day, she felt closer to him. Sometimes her heart beat so fast when he was near she was positive she was falling in love with him.

But it didn't seem to be enough. Every day, large parts of Rosevine were still dying; a reminder that all was still not well.

Chapter Sixteen
To Leave or to Perish

Two days before the wedding, Tangi sat on the windowsill, staring out into the magnificent garden — the rolling lawn, the birdbaths, and glittering leaves that hung from the rose tree outside her window.

Then, right before her very eyes, something terrible happened.

The leaves she'd been admiring suddenly curled up, let go of their twig and floated to the ground, dead. Then a rose dried out, its petals crinkling. Within just minutes, the branches were bare.

Enveloped by sheer black fright, Tangi jumped from the windowsill and paced around the room as she wrung her hands. This was it. Rosevine was a few hours from disappearing, and she couldn't do anything. The past few days she'd come to appreciate and like Daryle more, but the spark she so much wished for still wasn't there. She'd been wishing and believing as much as she could, but it didn't seem to work.

She had made promises she was afraid she might not be able to keep.

Fye entered the room, carrying clean folded sheets and Tangi's heart plummeted as she watched her place the bundle on the bed. She had shrunk even more since the day Tangi had arrived in Rosevine. And her friend's face was a mask of fear and pain. The same pain she'd seen on the faces of every Rosevien, including Daryle.

She bent down and engulfed Fye in a hug. "I'm sorry, Fye. I so much want to save you, all of you. I like Daryle very much, but it doesn't seem to be enough. Everything is still dying."

Fye broke the embrace and gazed up at her. "It's not your fault. You just can't force love."

A knock came from the door.

"Come in," Tangi said.

Daryle cracked the door open. "Tangi, you should come down. There's something you might want to see."

"What is it?" She prayed it was not more of Rosevine's disintegration. She couldn't bear anymore.

"You better come and see for yourself."

She followed him down the stairs, through the entrance hall, and out the door.

Outside, Tangi clutched her chest and her eyes grew wide.

There, squirming in a guard's solid grip, stood a person she had thought she'd never see again: Selma.

Tangi drew closer to Daryle. Her heart tightened in response to the fear she used to experience every time she was in Selma's presence.

She looked up at Daryle with wide eyes. "What ... what—how did she get here?"

He put an arm around her shoulders to steady her. "Don't be afraid of her, Tangi. She can't do anything to you anymore. The reason she ended up here is because you had poured too many teardrops into the ditch. You poured in four instead of two. Because of that, it took a while before the pond could disappear."

"But Selma wasn't even there when I left." How could she ever move on with her life when the woman who had destroyed her past succeeded to slip into her future too?

"I was watching the day you left and saw her." Daryle spoke in a low voice, close to her ear. "She'd come back to collect a tin in which she kept money. When she left your uncle's farm, it had been in a hurry and she didn't have a chance to retrieve it from where she'd hidden it. The day you left, she watched you and your uncle at the pond. She waited until your uncle went back into the compound, then she dived in. I didn't want to worry you. That's why I didn't tell you."

"How did the guard find her?"

"She was captured at the gate. When she touched the diamond, her fingerprints set out a secret alarm in the guard's cabin because the fingerprints did not belong to a Rosevien."

"Why did he bring her here?"

"My father and I thought you might want to say something to her before she goes to the dungeon. Now go down there and tell her everything you never had a chance to say." He winked at her.

Daryle was right. There was one question she always wanted to ask Selma. Before coming to Rosevine, she'd stood up to Nona and Maria. Maybe now was the time to stand up to the woman who had hurt her so much as a child. A sudden boldness surged through her body when she thought of what Selma had done.

She squared her shoulders and walked down the steps. Then she came face to face with her. Selma stared at her with empty eyes. Strangely, unlike Tangi, Selma had not changed. Except for peeling skin and dry lips from the desert heat, she was still the same age as in Mimbeye. Fye had mentioned that only Roseviens changed age when they crossed the border between Rosevine and the other world.

Selma searched Tangi's face in confusion. She clearly had no idea who she was.

"You don't remember me, do you? But how would you? I don't have a shorter leg anymore. That's what you used to make me feel small, wasn't it?"

Selma stopped fighting the guards and gaped at her. Their eyes locked. Selma's looked as if they'd drop out of her head any second. Then she leaned forward, as far as the guard would let her—which was not much—and opened her mouth to speak. "Tangi?" She made a pitiful attempt at looking excited. "Is it really you? I'm so happy to see you. You're all grown. How did that happen?"

"I'm not here to answer any of your questions. I came down to ask you one thing. What did I ever do to you to make you treat me so harshly? What kind of person treats a child like you treated me?"

Selma flinched, broke eye contact.

Tangi shook her head. "How could you live with yourself? I was just an innocent child, and you knew how my leg would hurt when you ordered me about. You did it anyway. Did I ever do anything to you?"

"No," Selma mumbled under her breath.

Tangi tilted her head to one side. "And yet you were so cruel to me. I need to know why."

Selma lifted her head and glared at Tangi. She clenched her fists. "Why? Because I hated you, that's why! If you hadn't shown up, Thomas would have fallen in love with me. You ruined everything. All he cared about was you and your stupid leg."

Lisa had told Tangi it was just about them not wanting to look after her and her sisters. It shocked her to realize that Selma had other plans. "You wanted my uncle to fall in love with you? Really?"

Selma dropped her head again. This time, she was in the weaker position. "Forget what I said."

"No," Tangi shot back. "I won't. I won't, because it's what made you treat me so bad. I don't know you that well, Selma, but I do know my uncle. I'm pretty sure I wasn't the reason he wasn't interested in you. It's all because he is a kind and caring man. I'm also sure he knows an evil person when he meets one. He deserves so much better than you. I don't ever want to see you again." She stepped back and looked at Daryle.

He moved to her side, then turned to his guard. "Take her away. My father and I will let you know what to do with her." A muscle quivered at his jaw.

The guard nodded and dragged Selma away.

Selma craned her neck to look back at Tangi. "I didn't mean to say all that. Tangi, tell him to let me go." She struggled, flailing in the guard's grip. "Hey, where are you taking me? Let me go!"

Tangi laid her head on Daryle's chest and closed her eyes. The sound of his heartbeat told her how much she meant to him. It saddened her that she had the power to break it without mean-ing to.

After a while they walked back to the castle.

Tangi weaved her fingers through his. "I don't understand. How did she survive, if she arrived the same day as I did? That desert heat was deadly."

"My father and I decided that after what she'd put you through, death would be too easy a way out. She should suffer like you did. Without knowing, she was led to a secret spring in the desert. Drinking from it kept her alive."

"What will happen to her now?"

"She'll go to the dungeon."

"You actually have a dungeon in Rosevine?" It was hard to imagine any person in Rosevine doing something that would get them arrested.

"Yes, in the dead part of Rosevine, and she will be the only resident there."

Tangi could not think of a better punishment. Day in, day out, all by oneself, isolated from everyone else. She had felt like that all her life, and even more when she'd met Selma.

"What will happen to her if —"

Daryle didn't let her finish. "If Rosevine perishes, she will find herself back in the desert, and this time, there will be no water or food to keep her alive. She'll suffer a slow and painful death. If Rosevine is restored, she won't be thrown into the desert but she'll remain in the dungeon for the rest of her life."

Tangi didn't care what happened to Selma, as long as she didn't have to see her again. A thought crossed her mind. "Do you know anything about my sisters?" She'd thought about them a few times, wondering what had become of them.

"They got expelled from boarding school for sneaking out of the hostel at night. Your uncle refused to take care of them any longer, so they are living with one of your aunts. The one you attacked at your father's funeral."

Tangi's cheeks flooded with heat. "You know about that?" Of course he did. He knew everything.

He laughed. "I do, and I think she deserved it. Let me just say, your sisters regret taking your uncle for granted."

Tangi wasn't happy that Nona and Maria now lived with mean Aunt Dabina. She wouldn't wish that on any one. But she was glad Uncle Thomas could have his peace.

As Tangi and Daryle reached the top of the steps, Fye opened the door.

"The king and queen would like to see you in their private living room." She sounded agitated.

A flicker of apprehension coursed through Tangi. It was only a matter of time before the king and queen stopped ignoring the signs and started preparing themselves for the moment they would all perish.

They walked side by side down the hallway. "Daryle, I'm so sorry about this."

He pushed open the doors to the living room. "You don't have to be sorry. I knew from the start you might never fall in love with me."

He was wrong. After all the time they had spent together and she had gotten to know him, she *had* actually fallen in love with him. But apparently not enough for Rosevine. Now she had given them hope, which was fast disappearing, just like their land.

The king and queen were already waiting for them. Queen Lorea's eyes were empty. Tangi had never seen her look less than perfect before. Today, a curly strand of her black hair had freed itself, and there were dark circles around her eyes.

The grey in King Smineon's hair seemed to have multiplied. Although his shoulders were hunched, his eyes still mirrored determination. The same expression she saw in Daryle's.

"Thanks for coming, Tangi. I know it must be a hard morning for you after seeing Selma."

Tangi sat down next to Daryle on a sofa not too far from the king and queen. "I'm doing all right, thank you." Daring to question Selma when she hadn't before had been good for her. She could move on with her life now, or whatever was left of it.

"I'm going to be straight here." King Smineon clasped his hands in front of him. "We can't pretend Rosevine isn't over. We have to accept it. The people deserve to know so they can say their goodbyes. We might all never live to see the day after tomorrow. I say we call off the wedding. It's too late to change anything."

Daryle looked at Tangi, and so did the king.

"I know what I feel for Daryle might not be

enough to save Rosevine, but I still want to marry him tomorrow. I think I'm in love with him."

"Tangi," Daryle said. "I know you want to help, and we are all grateful to you, but what you feel for me can't be enough, otherwise we would already be able to see the signs."

Queen Lorea touched her son's knee and interrupted. "We appreciate that you wanted to help us save the kingdom." She stopped talking as her lips trembled.

King Smineon continued for her. "The reason we want to do this now is so we can save you. We want to give you a chance to go while you still can. If you're still in Rosevine on the last day, you'll be stuck and will perish like everyone else here. You don't deserve that."

Tangi bit her lip. If she gave up now, she'd go back to the other world a failure. Even if they didn't hold anything against her, she would never forgive herself. The thought of what could have been would be stuck in her mind for as long as she lived. "What if my love for Daryle grew tomorrow? If I go, we will never know."

"What if it doesn't?" Queen Lorea asked. "Then it would be too late for you."

"I don't want to go back."

Daryle looked Tangi deep in the eyes. "We have made all the necessary arrangements so you will never again suffer the way you did before coming here. Of course, you'll always be an outsider, and people will make you feel it, but no one will ever hurt you physically again. And you know what?"

"What?" Tangi's throat constricted.

Daryle's gaze didn't leave her face. "We broke a few rules for you. When you go back, you'll be thirteen again—we couldn't get out of that—but you'll keep your new leg. You'll be normal and healthy. I found a way to contact your uncle, and he's anxious to see you. We made him promise to never again let anything happen to you."

Queen Lorea crossed the room to a desk in the corner and returned holding a carved wooden box. Sitting down, she placed the heavy box in Tangi's hands.

"What is this?" Tangi opened it and a piercing light flooded out. She squinted to lessen the sharpness. When her eyes had adjusted, a soft gasp escaped her. The burgundy silk-lined box was filled to the brim with water pearls and diamonds.

Queen Lorea stroked Tangi's hair. "These should take care of your financial needs for the rest of your life. They will make all your dreams come true. Go to the best schools, have the best clothes and shoes, and get whatever you will ever need or want."

Tangi touched a smooth, light-pink pearl. "I can't take this. It's too much."

King Smineon stood. "You have to, Tangi.

Rosevine will never have a future, but it will all be worth it if you create one for yourself." He sighed and straightened his shoulders. "I'll go and get ready to announce your departure." He walked out of the living room.

Queen Lorea reached out her hand and lifted Tangi's chin. "Your life can begin today."

How could Tangi begin a life when theirs was just about to end? "Do I really have to go?"

"Yes," Daryle said, his voice grained, not as smooth as usual. "Your mother would have wanted you to do this. We do, too. After the announcement my father will be making in an hour, you have a chance to say goodbye. And I'll see you off tonight to make sure you arrive at the gate safely."

After Queen Lorea left the living room, Daryle moved closer to Tangi. "I love you so much and, as you know, my love will last forever. I want you to be happy. I want you to live."

"The happiest I've ever been is here. I'll never get this back again. And I do love you, Daryle."

Daryle pulled her to him and held her. "I wish things could be different."

Tangi cleared her mind of all thoughts except one. She lifted her head to look in Daryle's face. "Maybe they can be different. You told me that I can have whatever I want, as long as I wish for it and believe it." She rose from her seat, speaking animatedly. "Why don't you do that? I know Rosevine can never be saved, but what about you and the people of Rosevine? You could wish yourself out of here and come with me to start a new life in another world."

Daryle's head drooped dejectedly. The excitement Tangi had been hoping for didn't register on his face. "I'm afraid that can never happen. That's the one limit we have to wishing. Rosevine is not just a land. Rosevine is us. No matter where we go, when it perishes, so will we. It's something we can never escape. But since only your mother was Rosevien and not your father, you can."

So that was it. They had no way out. Tangi felt shattered. "I'm so sorry, Daryle."

"You don't have to be. I am sorry that you have to go back to the other world. Don't worry about us. We had a long time to prepare ourselves for this. Every time someone shrank or a petal died, we knew the end was near. Please go back."

Tangi blinked away the tears and turned on her heel, ready to leave the room. There was nothing left to say, to be done.

When Daryle thought she had left, he dropped his face in his hands.

Tangi stood in the doorway watching him. It crushed her to see him suffer like that, lose all hope. When he hurt and she felt it too, wasn't that love? What more was needed?

Back in her room, she stood at the window. Everything was still and silent. Not a bird sang. No wind rustled the leaves. Nothing. It was as if Rosevine had been frozen in time. She dreaded the announcement and seeing all the crushed faces.

In a daze, she showered under the small waterfall in her room and then dressed.

*

On a high balcony on one side of the castle, Tangi stood between King Smineon and Daryle. Queen Lorea stood on the other side of her husband. Eager and hopeful faces gazed up at them. They obviously hoped King Smineon would say something that could still save them.

King Smineon cleared his throat. "I'm sure you all know what I'm going to confirm right now. I'm sorry to tell you this, but Rosevine cannot be saved. There will be no wedding tomorrow. Princess Tangi will leave tonight."

Tangi looked down at the broken faces. Furrowed brows, pained expressions, and wounded eyes met hers.

Queen Lorea suppressed a sob.

After the announcement, Tangi went down to say goodbye to the people she had come to love and accept as her family.

King Smineon, Queen Lorea, Daryle and Tangi had one final meal together, then she went to say goodbye to Fye and Joe at their home. Fye opened the door and looked up at Tangi with trembling lips and red eyes.

Sitting together at the kitchen table, Fye said, "I can't believe after tomorrow it will be as if we had never even existed."

Although it had been thirty days, to Tangi it felt like months. The pace of time really was different in Rosevine. "I know. I wish there was something else I could do."

"The most important thing is you wanted to help."

Tangi stayed with Fye until Joe came home looking haggard. His job as caretaker was over, but he still felt responsible for making sure nothing got destroyed by one of the Roseviens in a moment of frustration and pain.

Tangi and Fye hugged and cried as they said goodbye. Then she left to go back to the castle.

*

Tinsel landed outside in front of the castle. He had come to fly Tangi and Daryle to the gate.

King Smineon and Queen Lorea stood in the doorway, gazing after them as they walked through the moonlight toward Tinsel.

Daryle helped Tangi onto Tinsel. Stroking the enormous bird's feathers, she thought back to her first date with Daryle, how afraid she was. She also remembered Daryle, how she'd barely known him then. Back then she had only felt friendly feelings toward him. Now, with her hand wrapped around his, there was nothing that would have made her happier than to stay in Rosevine and marry him. Without a future left for them, nothing would ever be fine again.

"No more talking?" Tangi asked Daryle. They would part in a few minutes, and she wanted to hear his voice as much as she could for the last time.

He wrapped his arms around her, and Tangi cuddled closer to him. "There's so much I want to say to you, but there isn't enough time."

They didn't talk anymore. Instead they just enjoyed each other's warmth, talking without any words.

When Tinsel landed at the gate, they let go of each other and climbed down. On the ground, Daryle pulled Tangi closer to him and kissed her swiftly on the lips. It was her first kiss, and when he pulled away, she kept her eyes closed for a little while longer as the tips of her fingers tingled.

"I love you," he said softly. "Never forget that."

She opened her eyes. "I love you too. If I didn't know it before, I do now. When you kissed me just now, my knees went weak. It felt really good. That should mean something, don't you think?"

Daryle sighed. "I can't risk your safety. It's

ten o'clock now. If you don't walk through that gate by midnight, you'll be stuck here. If what you feel for me were enough, Rosevine would feel it. Please, you have to go. I can't go out of the gate with you, but there will be a guard waiting for you on the other side. He'll take you to a pond. Goodbye, my love."

Tears flooded her eyes, and hard as she tried, she couldn't blink them away. "I'll miss you."

"I'll miss you much more. Now go on. Don't make this too hard." Daryle's voice was soft.

Tangi looked over at Tinsel, who gazed directly at her, his dark round eyes gleaming. There was deep understanding and sadness in those great eyes. Tinsel nodded; Tangi did the same. Then she left them standing there as she walked the few steps to the gate. She clutched her bottles of tears and the box of diamonds and pearls, the only thing to remind her Rosevine ever existed.

When she reached the gate, she looked back at Rosevine. The roses on the trees glowed faintly, as did Tinsel's white feathers. Daryle stood next to him with his arms straight at his sides.

Tangi waved at them, then touched the diamond handle. The gate swung open for her. Without looking back, she walked through. As soon as she stepped outside the gate, her heart went cold and empty. She laid the flat of her right hand over her chest and gasped for air.

"Princess Tangi." The same guard who had escorted Selma into Rosevine stood in front of her. "Are you ready?"

Of course she wasn't. She would never be ready. "Yes."

A lamp appeared in his hand. "We better get going then." He walked ahead of her, and she followed.

The longer they walked through the desert, the more her head spun, and she thought she might faint. She stopped and bent over to catch her breath. "I can't get air," she panted. "Can we rest for a while?"

"We'll be there very soon. Can you walk just a little bit more?"

"I don't know." Tangi sank down onto the warm soft sand and sat there with her head in her hands. She yielded to the compulsive sobs that shook her and hot tears slipped down her cheeks.

The guard paced back and forth, asking over and over if she was all right.

When her tears finally turned into nothing more than sniffles, the guard extended a hand and helped her up. "Are you okay to go now?" he asked.

Tangi looked back in the direction of the gate. She couldn't see it from where she was, and it caused her stomach to cramp. "I can't do this. I need to go back."

The guard looked at her as if she was going

crazy. "You can't go back there. You know what will happen tomorrow. I'd leave if I were you; save yourself." He lifted the lamp and squinted at a pocket clock. "It's ten thirty now. You won't have enough time to say any more goodbyes."

"I know." She started to walk back. "I'm not going to say goodbye. I'm going to stay." She picked up her pace.

"Princess Tangi, please wait," the guard shouted from behind her, running to catch up. "Prince Daryle told me to make sure you leave. He wants you to be safe."

Tangi slowed down and faced him. "I know you're doing your job, but please understand that I have to do this. Leaving would be a mistake."

"But you can't save Rosevine. Not much could change within a day."

"You don't know for sure. Please take me back to the gate."

The guard's lips parted. He wanted to say something, but the doubt in his eyes was so strong, Tangi saw it even in the dim light. His shoulders sank lower. He had given in. "If that's what you want."

"Thank you so much. We'd better hurry. Maybe Daryle and Tinsel haven't flown off yet."

"I'm afraid they have already, but don't worry. I'll get you back to the castle. But we have to start with going in the right direction."

"What do you mean?"

He gave her a toothless grin. "You're headed in the wrong direction. This way." He turned in a half circle, and Tangi followed him.

The guard did find a way to get her back to the castle, with his own version of Tinsel — rougher feathers and less comfort. But the most important thing was that Tangi now stood outside the doors of the castle. It was thirty minutes to midnight, and there was no more turning back. She didn't regret a thing. She belonged here, and if it meant going down with Rosevine, she was ready.

She knocked. A few seconds later, the doors flew open and Daryle stood in front of her, his eyes widened with astonishment.

"Tangi, what are you doing here?"

"Daryle, we have a whole day left. We don't know for sure if tomorrow would be the day. If there's even a little chance that I could save Rosevine, I want to take it."

He moved aside to let her enter. "I can't believe you're doing this. I can't let you do it."

Tangi stepped closer to him. "It's not your choice. I want to do this. I'm going to marry you tomorrow. I love you. That's why I came back."

Daryle touched her cheek. "Tangi, I'm so worried about you. I don't want anything to happen to you, but I want to marry you more than anything."

"Then let's do it. Don't worry about me. Our love story might end tomorrow, or it might last forever. And even if we can't save Rosevine, at least we'll spend a final day together. For me, that's worth everything." She kissed him.

"You do know my parents will rush you out of here as soon as they find out, right?" He cocked an eyebrow.

"Then let's not wake them. Tell them in the morning that I'm back and the wedding will take place."

"I don't think they're sleeping, but if our wedding is going to happen, you might be right. You better go and get some sleep."

"That's a good idea." Tangi climbed the stairs to her room. "I do love you, Daryle. Maybe tomorrow, you'll be able to see it."

"And I love you, more than anyone could ever love you." He blew her a kiss.

Chapter Seventeen
The Last Day

"Wake up, Tangi. It's your wedding day," Fye said as she shook her awake.

Tangi's eyes opened. "How did you know I'm back?"

Fye fussed around her, smoothing the duvet and fluffing the pillows. "Daryle notified everyone before the sun rose. I'm glad you're still here—although I do think you're crazy, too."

"I'll only know if that's true by the end of today."

Fye sat next to her and looked at her with hope-filled eyes. "Maybe when you say 'I do,' everything will change for the better."

Tangi's eyes filled with tears and she swallowed the lump in her throat. "I want to believe that so much."

"Come on, get out of bed. We have a lot to do before the ceremony."

For a person who wasn't sure whether she would make it past this day, Fye was pretty cheerful. Maybe it was better to have faith than dread the future, or the possible lack of it.

Tangi rubbed her hands together. "We better

get started then." She jumped out of bed, hurried to the closet and pulled out her wedding gown. She had finally wished it right. The gown was beautiful—a dream of satin, pearls, and sequins.

Fye ran her flat palm across the delicate material. "Wow, you did a fantastic job. I'm impressed."

"Well, I learned from the best."

After she got back last night, Tangi had sat on her bed and pictured her wedding gown in excruciating detail. She'd failed three times. The fourth time, she'd opened her eyes and found the gown spread out on the bed next to her. It had worked because she had known exactly what she wanted—to marry Daryle. Leaving him had shown her how much she needed him.

Tangi took a quick shower while Fye went down to the kitchen to get her something small to eat and drink. After she was out, towel draped around her body, she peered out of the window. All the pain of her past was gone, of not being loved by anyone except her father and Uncle Thomas. Outside the window, Roseviens showed her their love as they scurried here and there, preparing for her wedding. They all showed true happiness despite the kingdom's obvious decay.

Flamingos cleared the rivers, lakes and bubbling brooks of dead leaves and twigs. Butterflies of pink, yellow, lavender and blue adorned the fences with countless roses.

"Everyone wants to make this day special for you and Daryle."

Tangi turned around to see Queen Lorea standing in the room. She wore a jade floor-length dress and her ears, neck and wrists dripped with diamonds. The dark circles that had framed her velvet brown eyes yesterday had disappeared; her skin was once again flawless. She closed the door.

"Thank you for coming back and sacrificing so much for us."

"I wanted to make sure I tried everything. And I love Daryle. I just hope that today everyone will get to see it."

Queen Lorea gave a little shrug. "If it doesn't happen, it would still be a beautiful farewell party for all of us. I just wanted to thank you."

When Queen Lorea left, Tangi saw two roses shrivel and die, and her heart almost went with them.

She shook her head. There was still hope.

Tangi shared her breakfast with Fye and they talked about how it would be if, after today, Rosevine still existed, and how wonderful it would be to see all the roses in bloom again.

"You know what the most wonderful thing is?" Tangi said.

Fye blew over her hot tea, sending the steam streaming in Tangi's direction. "What?"

A smile tipped the corners of Tangi's mouth.

"I will be married to Daryle. I'll have my own happy ending."

"It would not only be yours. That happy ending will belong to all of us." Fye sighed. "It would be so great to have my normal height back."

"I definitely want that for you too. That's why I'm here. For all of you."

*

Tangi's boat took them to the chapel. It looked beautiful, decorated with colorful flowers from her garden, beads and ribbons.

The boat glided like a soft cloud over the petal-strewn river. Forget feeling like a princess; right now, she felt more like a queen.

Everything sparkled. If it was beautiful when she had first arrived here, now it was dazzling, even if the green had faded from most of the leaves. It might mean death to the Roseviens, but it reminded her of autumn in Mimbeye.

Reds, oranges, and fading greens colored the leaves on the trees surrounding the white chapel. The air was fresh, and her thin veil swayed in the gentle breeze. A perfect day for a princess wedding. Some people gathered outside, waiting to see what would happen. They probably couldn't fit inside the chapel. She waved to them and stepped inside, followed by Fye.

The chapel was packed with white roses, flickering candles, and silk bows.

Tangi lifted her eyes, and from behind the veil she saw Daryle, standing at the altar. He looked handsome in a gold and olive-green kaftan with intricate and elaborate embroidery. His golden crown finished off the look.

His eyes didn't leave her face as she glided down the aisle toward him. With every step she took, she wished she would be able to make today a happy day. Not just for him but for all the Roseviens.

Even though she was trying to be brave, all eyes pointed to her, and everyone was expecting her to save them. Glancing at the expectant faces caused the knot in her stomach to tighten.

A cold shiver ran down her spine. What was she doing? Making promises she couldn't keep? Every muscle in her legs signaled her to run away. But it was too late. There was nowhere for her to go now. No matter where she would be in Rosevine, she would suffer the same fate as the people she would be letting down. She had to try.

Tangi focused on Daryle and finally she stood opposite him.

"It's all right," he mouthed.

She gave a slight nod. She wanted to believe him.

The priest cleared his throat and wiped the sweat off his forehead. Tangi noticed his hands trembled as he twisted them together.

"We ... are gathered to—" he started, then licked his lips. "We are gathered here to witness the marriage of Princess Tangi and Prince Daryle."

A sudden ringing in her ears made it hard for her to hear the words that followed.

"Will you, Princess Tangi, take this man to be your lawfully wedded husband?"

Daryle touched her hand and gazed at her with a big smile.

"Princess," the priest repeated, "will you take this man to be—"

"I do," she said in a voice just loud enough for Daryle and the priest to hear.

The priest asked Daryle the same question and he answered the same way.

"Prince Daryle and Princess Tangi, I now pronounce you man and wife. Daryle, you may kiss the bride."

Daryle lifted her veil, and their lips met.

When they parted, silence filled the chapel and everyone stared out the large windows. This was the moment they had waited for. Frozen, Tangi and Daryle looked outside, desperately hoping the kingdom would blossom. If she wasn't Daryle's true love, things would worsen. If she was ...

She froze when a strong wind came in and roughly swayed the branches of the tree by the window. The leaves curled up and dropped to the ground. Everyone jumped from their seats and the priest disappeared through the back exit.

Daryle grabbed her hand. They watched the people outside run for cover.

"Calm down, everyone." King Smineon's voice was calm. "It will be a few hours still before ... before. Please don't go out now. It's too dangerous. Let's just wait here for a while."

Everyone sat back down, but Tangi picked up on the shuffling of feet and soft crying. Outside, the sky darkened, a slanting grey shower started to pour, and thunder rocked the small chapel as if in anger.

Tangi and Daryle sank into their seats and listened to the rain drumming on the chapel's roof.

"I'm sorry I couldn't help. I gave you false hope."

"Ssh." Daryle pulled Tangi to him. "There's something else I want to try. I don't know if it will work."

"There's nothing else we can do, Daryle." She started to cry. "I've let everyone down. It's over."

"It's over only when we've tried everything. I love you, Tangi, and I hope this will work."

He dug into his pocket and pulled out a ring. He pushed it onto her finger.

Tangi stared at it. Recognition hit her, and tears spilled from her eyes and dripped onto her hand. "This was my mother's ring," she said. "I lost it a long time ago."

Before she could speak again, a warm glow flowed through her body and joy bubbled up inside of her. She knew then that her love for Daryle had been recognized. The ring proved to her they were made for each other.

"Oh, Daryle, I feel it! I love you so much."

A flash of light exploded outside. Then, like in the dream Tangi had had in Mimbeye, the rain stopped just like that, the sun poured out its rays, and the dead leaves started unfurling back to life.

The chapel filled with applause.

"They did it!" someone shouted. The words echoed from all the Roseviens and they hugged, laughed, and skipped around with joy.

"It's happening. I think Rosevine is saved." Tangi looked down at the ring in amazement.

Daryle lifted her chin and kissed her again. This time his kiss caused the pit of her stomach to swirl.

When they stopped kissing, they found laughing, smiling people surrounding them, waiting to congratulate them. Some of them were even crying for joy.

Tangi hugged Queen Lorea first.

"I guess we'll have many more parties after all," Queen Lorea said, and Tangi laughed.

When Queen Lorea let her go, King Smineon also engulfed Tangi in a tight hug. Then he broke the embrace and turned her to face a large flat screen propped up against one wall of the chapel. On the other side of the screen was Uncle Thomas, in his sitting room. Tangi ran to it. For the second time that day, the room quieted.

"I'm so proud of you for the choice you've made to stay there, my dear girl." He wiped his eyes with a handkerchief, and Tangi wiped her own. "I wanted you to come home, but they needed you more. I hope to see you again someday. Daryle promised to find a way for me to come and visit. Never forget that I love you."

"I love you too, Uncle," Tangi said, hiccupping.

The screen blanked. For a time, Tangi just stared into its depths. Seeing Uncle Thomas had made her miss him even more, but she knew without a doubt that this was her home.

After all the congratulations, Tinsel appeared outside the chapel, his feathers glittering. He had come to pick them up. Tangi thought she saw him wink at her.

Daryle helped her into the seat. Then Tinsel rose up into the clear blue sky, and everyone down below waved at them.

Tangi cuddled up to her husband and closed her eyes. "I can't believe that someone can be this happy. I'm where I want to be."

Daryle kissed the top of her head. "I'm glad you have arrived, my love."

Opening her eyes a short time later, Tangi

looked about. "Where are we headed? This is not the direction to the Hall Of Celebrations."

"Rosevine is still not completely restored. We're headed to our new home to make sure that happens. By this evening, all the roses would have bloomed and by tomorrow morning, there will be no shrunken people in Rosevine."

He pulled out the three bottles of tears.

A few minutes later, Tinsel landed in front of the castle that was once her grandparents' and now her own. It was completely repaired.

"I can't believe you rebuilt this whole castle in just a few weeks."

Daryle smirked. The dimple in his cheek made him look like a small boy caught doing something wrong. "Okay, I cheated a bit; just one little wish."

"Just one?" She bit her lip to stifle a grin.

Daryle took Tangi to her new secret garden, and together they poured the tears over the roses that grew there. When they had emptied all three bottles, Daryle led her to the side of the roof so she could look down. "Look what you just did."

"Wow." Blossoming flowers now covered the previously dead rose trees. The lakes and rivers sparkled crystal blue and the shades of green brought new life to Rosevine.

Tangi wiped her tears with the back of her hand. "This is the most beautiful place in all the world." She gazed up at him. "In all the universe."

"Your home. You paid for this with your tears. From now on, only happy tears will fill those beautiful eyes."

Tangi put her arms around his neck. "As long as you're with me, there will be no need for sad ones," she whispered. "Well, I guess this means forever, then."

He scooped her off the ground and into his arms and kissed the tip of her nose. "It has to be. After all we've been through, I wouldn't settle for anything less."

--The End--

CPSIA information can be obtained at www.ICGtesting.com
Printed in the USA
LVOW080200150912

298933LV00001B/34/P